LOGAN'S LEGACY

Having lost his ranch to jayhawkers, Henry Meade embroils the itinerant, ambitious Letty Dale in a plan. Together, they aim to convince a wealthy, old rancher that Letty is his long-lost granddaughter. The scheme involves them in dangerous enmities between local ranchers, life-threatening encounters with a rustling band, and battles with their own consciences. With Letty on the verge of being revealed as an impostor, it takes a perilous show-down with the rustlers to resolve matters.

Books by Terry Murphy in the Linford Western Library:

MISSOURI BLOOD TRAIL
HE RODE WITH QUANTRILL
CANYON OF CROOKED SHADOWS
SAN CARLOS HORSE SOLDIER
MIDNIGHT LYNCHING
THE HUNTING MAN
THE PEAKS OF SAN JACINTO

44139000257877

TERRY MURPHY

LOGAN'S LEGACY

Complete and Unabridged

LINFORD
Leicester

First published in Great Britain in 1999 by
Robert Hale Limited
London

First Linford Edition
published 2000
by arrangement with
Robert Hale Limited
London

British Library CIP Data

Murphy, Terry, *1962* –
Logan's legacy.—Large print ed.—
Linford western library
1. Western stories
2. Large type books
I. Title
823.9′14 [F]

ISBN 0–7089–5907–5

Published by
F. A. Thorpe (Publishing)
Anstey, Leicestershire

Set by Words & Graphics Ltd.
Anstey, Leicestershire
Printed and bound in Great Britain by
T. J. International Ltd., Padstow, Cornwall

This book is printed on acid-free paper

1

It was often said that the town of Raimondo was for losers. Maybe that was an unkind judgement, but there was justification for it. The ambitious rode on by, heading north for the opportunities offered by Dodge City, leaving the small town on the Canadian River to the hopeless and the helpless. Even the Raimondo Iron Works, the town's principal employer, was relegated to second-rate production due to the iron and available coal being of poor quality. Yet the inhabitants of Raimondo liked things the way they were. Enjoying the slow pace of life, they looked no further ahead than the next meal, the next drink. Even the drifters who came off the trail to tarry in the town for a day or two were dispirited men who added nothing but indifference to an already sterile atmosphere. Raimondo offered a peaceful existence that had to be paid for in boredom. But local folk welcomed the security of knowing that tomorrow would be the same as today and identical to yesterday. They were as apathetic as the town's dogs which lay throughout every day snoring and twitching on the sunbaked earth of the streets.

But every rule has its exception, and the blonde and pretty Letty Dale was proof of this in Raimondo. For as long as she could remember, which was something like eighteen of her twenty-three years, Letty had promised herself that one day she would be somebody. Letty didn't know what she would be, or when, but she had long ago made herself a promise which she intended to keep. Somehow she was going to reverse the bad fortune that had deprived her of all but the barest necessities during her early life. At times she had starved, but now her luck had shown a first but modest change for the better.

Letty had no complaint about the town. Raimondo had given her the first real home she had ever known. She had never learned who her parents were, having been raised by a sly-eyed Texan and his squaw wife who ran the agency on an Indian reservation. The Indian agent had been a violently cruel drunkard who had terrorized both the squaw and Letty. Tired of being an unpaid and badly treated skivvy, Letty had run away at the age of ten to spend the years ahead on many differing but dangerous trails. Out of necessity she had served an apprenticeship in the crafts of petty criminality. To achieve her ambition she was prepared to use these learned skills, but would not go so far as gunplay, or anything else that could result in others being physically harmed.

Letty had arrived in Raimondo a little over two years ago, homeless, penniless, and emaciated by hunger and hardship. Expecting to get the usual rebuff that was more or less guaranteed by her appearance, she had applied for work at the town's Portage Hotel. To her surprise, the proprietress, Mrs Nelly Kierney, gave her a job and took a motherly interest in her. The relationship between them had developed so well over the next few months that the hotel owner had unofficially adopted her.

There was sufficient transient traffic to support the hotel, and Letty worked hard, mainly waiting on tables in the dining-room. She was happy in the first real, undemanding relationship she had ever known.

Though comfortable and enjoying the novelty of wanting for nothing, Letty hadn't abandoned her dream of amounting to something. It was possible for her to do that by remaining in Raimondo. Already she was individually and hesitantly pursued by a group of hopeful suitors from the town's businessmen. Most persistent, and unfortunately inarticulate, was Frank

Berry, Raimondo's butcher. Berry was some fifteen years her senior, and probably one hundred times richer than she could ever hope to be, but Letty wasn't prepared to accept a mediocre existence in return for marrying a wealthy man. Aware that she would one day have to break the heart of Nellie Kierney by moving on, this was outweighed for Letty by the devastating prospect of a lifetime in sleepy Raimondo.

In addition to Frank Berry's shy but persistent attempts at courting her, Letty had had all kinds of offers from strangers she served food to as they dallied a short while in Raimondo. It was really pathetic to listen to inadequate men who had misused their own lives, boasting that they could help her make something of hers. When rejecting these dubious offers, Letty had never done so harshly. The usual kind of man who stopped by in this town had only a scrap of fragile dignity remaining. Letty shrank from depriving anyone of something so diminished but still very precious.

Yet now, as she brought out the first meals of the evening, she had to admit that the stranger sitting alone at the corner table was out of the ordinary. His long hair wasn't unusual except that it wasn't unkempt, and he was clean-shaven. The Navajo blanket vest he wore was unsoiled, his blue denim trousers were faded but clean, and the boots were polished and the heels were not run over at the sides. This neatness was out of keeping with the bum-like visitors Raimondo was accustomed to. The only presentable-looking guests the hotel had were drummers, and they were a strange breed who sat silently at tables mentally rehearsing their sales pitch for the morrow.

Even the heavy six-gun in a holster tied down with a whang string was somehow made less threatening by this man's appearance. Letty guessed that he was approaching middle-age, but she was pleased to notice that he was both handsome and interested in her. With it too early for her to be busy, she had been aware of him watching her intently as she had leisurely gone about her duties.

When she placed the meal on his table he thanked her in such a gentlemanly manner that she lingered when he continued speaking. Normally she would have moved away politely.

'I believe that I owe you an apology, miss,' he said with a friendly smile, 'for my rudeness in staring. It's just that, meaning no disrespect to this establishment, I am surprised to find someone like yourself working here.'

Speaking in a quiet, deeply masculine voice, he had the look of a gunslinger and the tongue of a lawyer. This was something that had Letty intrigued and wary. She'd met all kinds, relying on her agile brain to contend with them, but this man was different. Whatever he might be, he was far above the class of person she was used to.

'You make it sound different, mister,

but you're not saying anything I haven't heard before, too many times,' she told him, perhaps too abrasively, she noticed with a touch of regret.

'Again I must say that I'm sorry, miss. I can imagine that being approached must be annoying for you,' he sympathized. 'But I meant what I said about you being a cut above waiting on table.'

Liking him, Letty shrugged. 'I guess I should reply to that by saying that you are a cut above our usual guests.'

'There you are, we've exchanged compliments,' he said with a low, short laugh of genuine amusement. 'That surely must make us friends.'

'Which doesn't mean it's that almighty an occasion, mister. Come the morning you'll be riding on down the trail, and I'll still be here waiting on table.'

Letty was conscious of Mrs Kierney watching from the kitchen doorway. Her employer, her foster-mother as it were, was not checking on her work, but looking out for her welfare. When she went to the kitchen she would explain to Nelly that she'd been in conversation with a right gentleman.

'Now that may not be so, miss,' he said, pausing to study her intently for a long moment. Letty was embarrassed by the warmth that came to her cheeks. She knew that she just had to be blushing. The brilliant whites of his eyes contrasted by his deep tan, and their penetrating blueness unsettled her in a peculiar way. 'You see, I need you for something I've been planning for a long time. I see you as an ideal partner.'

An excited Letty felt certain this was the chance she had been waiting years for. Too thrilled to reply at once, she looked around the dining-room. Other guests were arriving to take tables. Enthralled though she was by him, she couldn't remain with this stranger for much longer.

'Are you interested, miss?' he enquired when she hadn't answered.

'I could be,' Letty answered guardedly. 'Is what you're speaking of legal?'

'That's kind of hard to define, miss,' he replied awkwardly. 'Out West here, there isn't much business that can be done fair and square. Could we meet up later this evening to discuss what I have in mind?'

Letty's enthusiasm cooled. Had he seen her as the capable, resourceful girl that she was, and interpreted her character wrongly? Life had been real tough in the past, and she'd done lots of things that she now repented, but if this man was an outlaw inviting her to join him in a crime spree across the country in a haze of gunsmoke, then she wanted no part of him. Even so, she didn't want to make a mistake and lose out by jumping to conclusions.

Bewildering herself by turning it all over in her mind, Letty said, 'There's a small bar in the lounge. I'll be serving drinks there with Mrs Kierney from around nine o'clock. If we're not too busy I could sit with you awhile.'

‘That will do fine, miss. It will make it easier if I say my name’s Henry Meade.’

Accepting his introduction with a nod, she turned away. Letty knew that the time would drag before she met him again and heard his scheme. She was reluctant to get too excited in case what he had to say would be disappointing.

Whatever, there was work to be done, and Nelly Kierney was paying her wages. Letty had to see to other diners who required serving, but as she took a few steps from him he asked for her name.

‘Letty Dale,’ she automatically replied.

It wasn’t until she was in the kitchen, filling a tray with plates of food passed to her by Tse Chi, the hotel’s oriental cook, that shocked realization came to her: Henry Meade had spoken in the Comanche language when asking her name. How could he have known? Unthinkingly she had confirmed for him that he was right by answering.

Worry overtook the pleasant anticipation of what he intended to offer her. Always having been a loner, it was unnerving to discover that someone knew something about her. Nelly Kierney had never enquired about her past, and Letty had never volunteered any information about herself.

'Someone you once knew, Letty?'

Nelly Kierney, her employer and friend, tried to make the question sound casual as Letty was carrying the tray out of the kitchen. But there was anxiety in the older woman's tone; a strong hint of possessiveness that made Letty's blood run cold. She was able to share something of herself in friendship, but would not let anyone own her, even Nelly, her benefactress. Maybe her departure from Raimondo was overdue!

She paused in the doorway, balancing the tray. 'No, I don't know him, but he wants to have a talk with me later.'

'I wonder why,' Mrs Kierney mused, glancing across the dining-room to where Henry Meade sat. 'It strikes me that he's probably a gunfighter. He's likely a dangerous man, Letty. As you know, we get all kinds in here.'

Making no reply, Letty went out of the kitchen. As she made her way to a table occupied by Milton Grainger, who owned the iron works, and an elderly man who was probably a client of Grainger's she noticed that Meade wasn't staring at her as before. Yet she felt that he was watching her every move, a fact which warmed her while paradoxically sending a chill down her back. The latter was caused by her fearing that Nelly Kierney could be right, and Henry Meade was a dangerous man.

'May I sit with him for a little while in the lounge if we're not busy?' she asked when back in the kitchen.

'Of course,' Nelly Kierney replied, generously and falsely. 'All I ask is that you take care, Letty.'

'You've no need to worry,' Letty said, sensing with horror that Mrs Kierney would have liked her to add the word 'Mother'.

Discovering that her friendship with the kindhearted older woman had suddenly become suffocating, and the hotel itself oppressive, the honest Letty accepted that the change in her feelings could well have been brought about by Henry Meade and the prospect of him taking her away from here.

Impatiently waiting, she was relieved when he was the first to enter the lounge that evening. Fetching him the rye whiskey he ordered, Letty sat down when he gestured for her to do so. A question had been building up inside of her for so long that she feared she would blurt it out so loudly that Nelly Kierney would hear it from her position in the far corner of the room.

Controlling herself, she eventually managed to ask quietly, although there was a noticeable tremor in her voice, 'How did you know?'

Immediately grasping what she meant, he shrugged his wide shoulders.

'You showed many signs of having been about Indians, miss.'

She didn't doubt that he was telling the truth. An experienced frontiersman knew such things. Meade had read the movements and mannerisms she had unconsciously taken on when playing with Comanche children before she was big enough to be put to work.

'When I was a child, my father, or father of sorts, was an Indian agent,' she said defensively.

'That figures,' Meade said with a satisfied nod.

'This has got something to do with what you want to talk to me about?' Letty said.

'It has everything to do with it,' he agreed. 'I'll put the whole thing to you, Miss Dale, and leave it to you to decide whether to go along with me or not. Does that sound fair to you?'

'I have nothing to lose by listening to what you have to say.'

Although she didn't show it, Letty was eager. What Meade was about to suggest had to be something really thrilling. Though he looked to be tough and capable enough to hold up trains and rob banks, Letty didn't consider him to be so coarse as to ask her to join him in that kind of violence. Whatever proposition he was going to put to her, Letty had already half decided to join him. Wanting to urge him to enlighten her, she watched Meade raise his glass to drink before going on.

'Normally I don't feel obliged to explain myself, Miss Dale, but sitting here with you I feel that I have to,' he began. 'I once knew better times. I had my own spread to go back to after the war. It was a fine ranch with a lot of good grazing and plenty of water. I spent more than two years building up my stock of beef, but I got hit by a bunch of Jayhawkers who took everything that I owned.'

'I'm sorry to hear that,' Letty commiserated.

'They sure put me up Salt River, miss, but I mean to get back to what I was, have my own place again,' he told her solemnly. 'Hear me out, Miss Dale, and then you can just walk away if you don't like what you hear.'

'I'm happy to listen,' Letty assured him with a weak little smile.

'There's a big ranch down Tolula way that's owned by an old guy named Danny Logan,' Meade started slowly. 'The way I hear it, Logan weren't much more than a saddle tramp riding a wagon when he came to the territory. Had himself a wife, daughter, and grandchild, a baby girl by all accounts. Seems like they were raided by redskins before they could get the roof on a sod shack he was building. Logan and his woman survived the attack, but the daughter was killed trying to defend her child, and the baby was snatched by the Indians. Now Logan's rich, and he knows he doesn't have much time left, so he's offering a reward to anyone who can find that grandchild. That reward is large enough to set me up with my own spread once more.'

Letty was shaken. She gasped, 'You don't think that I am the grandchild?'

'No, I sure don't,' Meade said with a shake of his head. 'If she was lucky, then that girl has been dead a long time, Miss Dale. If she's still alive, then she'd be too much of an Indian now to want to leave what she'd think of as her people.'

Mind racing in an effort to put what he was saying in order so as to be able to understand it, Letty failed. Knowing his subject well, probably having considered it from every angle, Henry Meade had assumed that she would have no problem with it. Normally quick-minded and proud of it, Letty was at a loss to know why she couldn't link what Meade was saying with herself. In desperation, she confessed that she had missed whatever point he was trying to make.

'None of this means anything to me.'

'My fault,' Meade acknowledged, raising both hands in token surrender. 'What I'm trying to put across to you is that though you may not be old Logan's granddaughter, there's no reason why you shouldn't become her.'

'You mean . . .' she croaked hoarsely, smitten by the audacity of what he was suggesting. Then she returned to being rational. 'No, it wouldn't work. Both you and me know that I'm not the granddaughter.'

'We do, but Danny Logan wouldn't,' Meade told her encouragingly. 'He'll know the way someone who's been with Indians acts, and you'd convince him without trying.'

Ashamed of herself, Letty found the scheme to be increasingly appealing. But at the same time it was ridiculous. How could she present herself to a complete stranger and convince him that she was close kin? She voiced her reservations to Henry Meade.

'You surely don't believe that we can ride up and announce that I'm his granddaughter? No man is going to believe that.'

'That would be a loco thing to do,'

Henry Meade concurred. 'I've got this whole thing thought out real sweet, Miss Dale. If you go along with it, we go to Tolula and have old Danny believe that it's him who finds you. He'll take the bait the way I plan to lay it. Then I move in to say how I brought you to him.'

Letty told herself that she should have known that the smart Henry Meade would have perfected the scheme. It still held immense appeal for her, but advance guilt had started to trouble her. Ready to seize any opportunity to flee from the greyness, the sameness, the endlessness of each and every day in Raimondo, she desperately wanted to say yes to Meade, but the conscience that had always guided her was uneasy.

'To do such a thing would be so deceitful,' she objected, willing Meade to agree and instantly quash the temptation she was finding it more and more difficult to resist.

But he made everything worse,

reasoning with, 'There's truth in what you say, but if you look at it sensibly, Miss Dale, you'll see that you'll be making it possible for an old man to die happy.'

'I'll be fooling an old man into dying happy,' Letty corrected Meade.

'Do any of us care what makes us happy, as long as we are happy?'

Unable to argue with that, Letty stayed quiet. Waiting for Meade to say something else, she made a deal with herself. If she found what he said next to be compelling, she would go along with the whole plan.

'We make Danny Logan happy, you inherit the DL Ranch, and I get my reward,' he said in a tone of reason. 'That way we all win.'

Other guests were entering the lounge now. A meek, fat little drummer and a tall, bony preacher-man, looked out of place among three border ruffians, each with the unmistakable manner of men who were on the run. Nelly Kierney didn't require her help to serve them.

It was a tempting offer. Being the owner of a large ranch was beyond her wildest dreams. It was trickery, she granted that, but those who have known injustice and hardship are driven by something different to the people who have had life easy. If Meade's plan was successful she wouldn't be depriving anyone of anything. She'd known one case of a rancher who had died with neither chick nor child to inherit what it had taken him a lifetime to acquire. People who had been squatting on the range had taken over the dead man's land and property, and rustlers had helped themselves to his cattle.

She earnestly enquired, 'Do you think it will work?'

'I know we can make it work, Miss Dale.'

'But I know nothing of ranching,' she protested. 'Will you stay and help me run the place when . . . when the time comes?'

Letty found that she couldn't bring

herself to say 'when the old man dies'. If she was going to go ahead with this, then she had to keep parts of it unreal. She was disappointed to see him give a negative shake of his head.

'As I said, I want a place of my own, Miss Dale. You won't have any problems. Danny Logan has an efficient foreman, a man named Charles Casson, and enough cowhands to take care of everything. All you'll have to do is relax and enjoy a life of luxury.'

This sounded real good to Letty, who found herself taking on the faith he had in his plan. She said dubiously, 'It would mean giving up my job and my home.'

'I know which I'd put my money on,' Meade remarked, looking around the less than auspicious hotel, displaying how unimpressed he was by the place.

He was right, Letty told herself. She was letting sentiment and emotion dissuade her from accepting the opportunity of a lifetime. Taking her leave of Nelly Kierney was a huge problem that she could solve easily. It was cowardly, but she would leave a note. She would thank her friend for everything, and try to explain why she just had to go.

'I'll go with you, but it will have to be tonight.'

'That's fine. I take it you can ride, Miss Dale?'

'I learned before I could walk,' she assured him proudly.

Her reply brought a grin to Meade's face. 'I guessed as much. I've got a spare horse, so you give me a time and I'll be ready to help you shake the dust of Raimondo off your boots.'

2

Though no truce had ever been called, there was an unspoken agreement between bitter enemies Dan Logan and Buck Woodward. Perhaps out of respect for Logan's age, Woodward always kept his men out of Tolula on Thursdays. The Running M boys, annoyed at constantly being bad-mouthed by the oldster, were likely to go on the prod if they came across Logan when they had a few shots of rye inside them. Not that they didn't have good reason. It wasn't their fault that their outfit hadn't lost a single steer, while Logan's DL Ranch and Rosie Kirby's Three Cs were losing out heavily to rustlers. The fiery Rosie made no public accusations; Sheriff Moses Basso continually declared that there was no evidence against Buck Woodward, but Dan Logan couldn't be dissuaded from openly declaring that the Running M was responsible for his losses. Folk with long memories were of the opinion that at the core of the present enmity was the residue from a threatened range war between Logan and Woodward twenty years ago. That was when Woodward had first moved on to the Running M. It had come close, but harsh words between the two hadn't erupted into gunplay.

Thursday was Logan's day for coming to town. Riding high on the specially raised seat of a buckboard, his grey hair flying wildly in a speed-generated breeze, the old man came in to pick up provisions for the week. He could have sent a hired hand on the errand, but he preferred to do his own picking and choosing. Anyway, he always liked to take back a little something special for his wife. She deserved everything he could do for her. Myrtle, bedridden these past four years, looked forward to her treat. It was the only highlight in what for her was a dreary week.

As he slowed the buckboard on reaching the edge of town, absent-mindedly exchanging a wave with Ned Reilly who stood outside of his forge, Logan deepened the lines in his forehead with a frown. Up ahead, outside of Ikey Kindler's general store where Logan was heading, a group of riders stood close to the rail to which their horses were hitched. They were talking and laughing in the raised-voice way young men have when they gather together. It was a sound that Dan Logan didn't like. One minute it would be pleasant enough, the next it could explode violently, usually to the detriment of some innocent soul who happened to be passing.

Tolula wasn't accustomed to menacing visitors such as these. Occasionally, the cowboys from local ranches, Logan's included, would go a bit too far, but Sheriff Basso soon took care of them. They'd sober up after a night in the calaboose, and get a stern warning from their bosses next day. Even Buck

Woodward was strict in that way.

Keeping the buckboard rolling, Logan wasn't afraid. He'd take on ten men and two grizzlies at the same time if needs be. But he had to be cautious these days. If anything happened to him, then Charles Casson, his dependable ramrod, could run things, but there would be no one to take care of Myrtle.

The men, all of them armed, fell silent to watch as he climbed down from the buckboard. There were mocking expressions on their tough faces; the superior attitude the young and arrogant adopt in the presence of the aged. Clustered together on the sidewalk close to the door, they turned their nearness into a threat by not giving way. A smell of liquor tainted the air.

Inwardly raging, Dan Logan eased past them. A long time ago, too long for him to contemplate happily, he'd have used an elbow into the nearest belly, and would then have enjoyed finishing what he had started.

Inside, Ikey Kindler's eyes, large and doleful as those of a fresh-born calf, greeted Logan before the store owner spoke in his customary funereal tone.

'Howdy, Dan. You pass them plug uglies outside? They're going to be trouble, you mark my words. This town can do without the likes of them.'

Eyes adjusting to the shadows inside of the store, Logan saw a young woman avidly studying a line of small, varied items on one of Kindler's shelves. Her pretty face was alive with excitement as she touched everything on the shelf in a childlike manner. She wore a calico dress of blue and white on a slender body that, though feminine, had a poised strength born of an outdoor life. Something about her caught and held Logan's attention, but he couldn't be sure what it was. There was a sweetness to her that was rare in these parts, but the attraction she held for him was more than that.

'Looks to me like they're about to ride out, Ikey.'

'I don't think so.' Ikey Kindler shook his head worriedly. 'They been drinking down at the Faro Wheel, and they've got bottles of red-eye outside there with them.'

'Buckaroos like them are just mouth, Ikey. They like shooting the breeze, that's all.'

The girl had a companion. A fine-built, handsome man, he was studying Kindler's stock of handguns. Logan detected that the man was just idling his time away in deference to the girl's enjoyment. He had a special way with him, as if his hard, muscular body encased a decency usually absent in his type. What type was he? A hired gun was Logan's guess. But that didn't explain what he was doing here with this girl. Both of them were strangers to Tolula.

'I got your order ready for you afore you rode in, Dan,' Kindler said glumly, like he was announcing the death of a mutual friend. 'I s'pose you want something special to take back for the little lady.' The storekeeper brightened up. 'Tell you what I've got out back, Dan, a lovely carpet, colours like you never seed afore. Had two of them shipped in from Turkey, would you believe. Ned Farrar bought one straightaway for the upstairs quarters at the Faro Wheel. The other one's yours if you want it.'

'Sure thing . . . ' Logan began, eager to see the carpet, but a squeal from the girl stopped him speaking and held him immobile.

Face glowing, she was holding up a pewter whale-oil lamp for her male companion to see. Voice vibrant, she cried, 'Oh, look at this, Henry. I remember this. Yes, we had one in the wag — ' Suddenly crestfallen, she fell silent. Unhappily, she replaced the lamp on the shelf.

'What is it, Letty?' the man with her enquired, full of interest. 'What were you going to say.'

Shaking her head sadly, she replied, 'I really don't know. It was as if I remembered something, but it was just a flash, then it was gone.'

Low down at the back of Dan Logan's head there began a strange, icy prickling that spread up slowly to cover his entire scalp. Maybe the girl couldn't recall where she had seen such a lamp, but he knew of one just like it that they'd used on the trek out and had since kept in the house as a memorial to those harsh times. He was aware that some visitors to the DL Ranch went away laughing at the way Myrtle and he had turned the lamp into an icon. That didn't worry Logan. As a man grew older he needed some visible link between his today and his yesterdays.

What he had just witnessed was too much to be dismissed as coincidence. Even so, Logan knew how easy it was to deceive yourself when you wanted something real bad. Maybe that's what he was doing. He was about to speak to the girl, although uncertain what he would say, what he should say, but Kindler called to him impatiently.

'I got other things to do, Dan, if you don't want to see this carpet.'

'I'm with you, Ikey,' Logan called, walking off but keeping his head turned a little so as to keep the girl in sight.

Though fair-haired and in every way a white woman, there was something about her lithe way of moving that just didn't fit. Everything about her was adding up to an equation in Logan's head that made him linger near her longer, despite the fact that Ikey Kindler's temper was becoming ragged.

Wrapping a swansdown boa around her neck she did a laughing twirl in front of her man friend. She put a cute little expression on her face as she peered at herself in a wall mirror that was overlaid with the wording of an advertisement for cocoa. Putting the boa back where she had found it, the girl picked up a loaf of corn pone, gave the man a nod that said she'd finished her fun and was ready to leave. The man paid Kindler for the bread and then the pair of them went out of the door. Logan moved reluctantly into the back room.

He bought the colourful carpet on sight and at the asking price. Kindler and Logan had known each other too long to bother with bartering. Anxious to get back on the street, hopefully for another sighting of the girl who had intrigued him so, he carried the rolled carpet under one arm while a puffing Ikey Kindler followed behind with his provisions.

Someone outside yelled something. This was followed by laughing and the sounds of movement. Kindler called to Logan, 'Let's bide our time in here awhile, till whatever's going on out there is settled down.'

Some sort of tomfoolery was taking place. It had to be the young ones Logan had seen on the way in acting up. Usually this mixture of high spirits and rye whiskey produced nothing more serious than bravado. That was something that Logan could ignore and go on his way.

'You may be getting old so that kids can scare the pants off you, but they sure ain't going to worry me,' Logan said with a grim chuckle.

But when he went out through the door he let out a bellow of rage as he saw one of the young strangers riding his buckboard. The others lined both sides of the street, yelling and shouting encouragement. Hurtling the four-wheeled carriage up and down the street, the driver, a hard-faced fellow with a drooping moustache, did sharp turns that threatened to tip the buckboard over. Logan's horse was covered in a white lather of sweat and dust, its mouth foamed frothily, and its legs buckled as the erratic manoeuvres put it under unbearable strain.

Unmindful of the danger to himself, Dan Logan ran out into the street, shouting, 'Stop, stop that, you danged guttersnipe!'

The old man stood in the centre of the road with both arms spread wide. The long grey hair gave him the look of a Biblical character calling upon God. But the Almighty must have been looking the other way as Logan's own buckboard came charging at him. The man up in the driving seat clearly expected Logan to leap out of the way, but the old man stood his ground. Reining the horse round hard at the last moment, the driver took drastic avoiding action, but the front corner of the buckboard caught Logan's shoulder.

Spun round by the impact, the old man fell on to his back in the dust. But Dan Logan was a game old guy, and he was half sitting up, pulling a Colt Peacemaker from inside of his jacket, and aiming it at the driver who was skidding the buckboard round crazily in a turn.

One of the cowboys on the sidelines, a wiry man as sly-eyed as a coyote, drew a silver-handled gun from a fancily decorated holster, and levelled it at Logan. Stepping out from a gap between buildings on the far side of the road, Sheriff Basso, a hard, fit figure though past middle age, took in the situation at a glance. Shouting what was either a warning meant for Logan, or a caution intended for the cowhand with the silver six-gun, the lawman brought up the rifle he was holding.

A shot rang out. Dropping his rifle, Moses Basso did a quarter turn before collapsing over a hitching rail, hanging there with his head dangling and blood pumping from a shoulder wound.

Smoke curled from the barrel of the cowboy's six-shooter as he lowered it to take aim again at Dan Logan. He was smiling as his finger tightened on the trigger.

He didn't have the chance to fire a second shot. Instead he fell dead as the man who had been in Ikey Kindler's store with the girl appeared, suddenly and surprisingly, a Colt. 45 in his hand.

Seeing his buddy fall, the driver angrily swung the buckboard so that it was heading straight at Logan, who was attempting to get to his feet. The old man wouldn't be quick enough, and the slashing front hoofs of his own horse were on course to smash him to smithereens when the man fired again, shooting the driver out of the seat.

As the driver hit the dirt head first, his neck breaking with a sharp crack, the girl in the calico dress came seemingly from nowhere as her companion had. As agile and graceful as a running deer, she kept pace beside the horse before swinging herself up on to it. Riding bareback, she tugged on one of the animal's ears with both hands. Veering, the charging horse and buckboard cleared the sitting Logan by inches.

But the drastic move by the girl was too much for the buckboard, which, with Letty still on the back of the horse, came up sideways on to two wheels. Then with a crash it went over on its side, sending up clouds of dust. The horse was wrenched over with it. The girl leapt off to land nimbly on her feet, but the horse fell heavily, legs flailing in the air, mouth wide open and teeth on display in a silent scream.

As it toppled, the buckboard caught the girl's companion a glancing blow. He went face down into the dust, the six-gun flying from his hand.

Rolling, the man came up on one knee, eyes scanning the ground for his gun. But it lay in the dust, yards from him, and the remaining three thugs were advancing on him, guns drawn. They came slowly, confident that they had all the time in the world to avenge their dead comrades.

The girl was helping Dan Logan to his feet. The old man made a pretence of not needing assistance, but he was forced to cling to her shoulder for a moment to steady himself. She looked to where her friend half-knelt, unarmed and facing three guns. She cried out in helpless anguish.

'Henry!'

Brought to their doors and windows by the commotion, the people of Tolula were careful to remain under cover as they looked out on the dramatic scene.

It was so quiet that the sound of the three men pulling back the hammers of their guns cracked as loud as rifle shots. Click, click, click.

The helpless man and the frantically worried girl exchanged quick glances that conveyed much. Then the tension was broken by the sound of Sheriff Basso sliding down from the rail to ground that was stained with his blood. What seemed nothing more than a brief diversion suddenly changed the whole situation.

Though severely wounded, the tough sheriff used one hand to grab the barrel of his dropped rifle. Swinging the weapon in an arc, he let go to have it soar through the air in the direction of the kneeling man. With that done, Moses Basso collapsed with a groan.

The man on one knee in the dust, rolled as he plucked the rifle out of the air. Taken by surprise, the three men who'd had him covered moved to change their aim. But a bullet from the rifle went in under the chin of one of them, exploding open the top of his head as it exited. Working the lever furiously as he continued to roll, the man fired again, the heavy slug doubling over a second man as it slammed into his abdomen. With only one of the troublemakers left, the man came up onto his feet, rifle held waist-high, ready to fire.

Nerve snapping, the last member of the gang of young guns began to run. He deliberately headed to put the fallen buckboard between the man with the rifle and himself. But the girl was too quick for him. Leaving Dan Logan's side she took one long pace then stuck out a foot to trip the fleeing gunman.

With his six-shooter still gripped in his hand, he fell sideways. The man's fall put his head and shoulders on view from behind the fallen carriage. In a split second, his jaw was shattered and ripped bloodily from his face by a slug from the rifle.

Five men lay dead. With the danger

over, people chattering excitedly moved out into the street. Kneeling beside Sheriff Basso, Ikey Kindler called out, 'Somebody fetch Doc Spencer.'

Dan Logan took a neckerchief from his pocket, unfolding it to wipe at his lined face as the man with the rifle walked past him. With a single shot the man released the writhing horse from its agony.

'I thank you for what you've done for me, stranger,' Logan said, holding out a gnarled hand.

'Henry Meade,' the man with the rifle introduced himself as he took the proffered hand.

Folk were crowding round now, commenting on the shoot-out, which was something rare in Tolula. Others were cutting the dead horse free from its harness and making arrangements to right the crashed buckboard.

'I said them ruffians would cause trouble,' Ikey Kindler complained as he came up. 'That's all they rode in here for, to get liquored up and raise mayhem. The doc says Moses ain't hurt too bad, Dan.'

'Thank the good Lord for that,' Logan said thankfully.

Kindler was studying the girl, who was coolly using a hand to brush dust from her dress. The store owner complimented her. 'I guess I ain't ever seen no bronc buster do what you just did, young lady.'

Accepting this praise with a polite smile, the girl looked to Meade, who told Logan and Kindler. 'This is Letty Dale. She's a bit shy, but she learned all her riding tricks from the Comanche when she was a little girl.'

Hearing this, Logan became animated. Twice moving his lips to speak but with no words coming out, he joined a group of townspeople to help put his buckboard upright. When it fell back on its four wheels with a crash, battered down one side but still serviceable, he came back to Meade and Letty.

'I'm mighty grateful to you, miss,' he said awkwardly, pushing his long grey hair from his face with a hand. 'My name is — '

Meade broke in, 'We know who you are, Dan Logan. I brought Letty all this way to see you.'

Again lost for words, Logan eventually managed to articulate, 'Are you saying . . . ?'

'I'm saying nothing, sir,' Henry Meade said, 'except that I think you may be interested in meeting this girl.'

Emotion taking him by surprise, Logan made a pretence of running the neckerchief over his face again, but covertly wiped his eyes with it. Looking down at his dead horse, he spoke sadly. 'He's been a good 'un over the years. Shame he had to go like this.' Raising his head to face Meade and Letty, he said, 'I'll get me another horse from the livery. Are you heading for somewhere in a hurry, Meade, Miss Dale?'

Henry Meade shrugged. 'We aren't in any rush.'

'In that case, I'd like it mighty fine if you'd both come out to the DL with me,' Logan said.

3

Big wasn't a sufficient description of the DL Ranch. At 75,000 acres in all, huge was better suited. But there were no fit words to describe the ranch house. It was a magnificent tribute to the enterprise of Dan Logan, who had exchanged a covered wagon for a sod hut, the sod shanty for a modest house, and then the house for a building that was a veritable palace. In the three days they stayed at the DL ranch house, Henry Meade learnt to admire the old rancher, and Letty grew close to Logan. On the pretext of wanting time to consider whether or not Letty was his long-lost granddaughter, Dan Logan asked Meade to join the round-up. Now, as Meade strapped his bedroll to the saddle, he learned the real reason for the request.

'I wouldn't say this, Meade, if I

didn't figure you were a man I can put trust in,' the rancher began, squinting into the sun rather than look at Meade as he broached a difficult subject. 'Knowing that this will stay just between the two of us, I want you on the round-up because I'm losing so many cattle that it can't go on.'

Meade buckled the last strap before asking, 'And you suspect your own men?'

'I didn't say that,' Logan retorted hotly, then calmed. 'Well, you're partly right, Meade. Seems like there's one or two rotten apples in the DL barrel.'

'Casson?' Meade questioned quietly.

'Land sakes, Meade! I'd need to be as blind as a post hole not to know if my own ramrod was robbing me. Charles Casson is the straightest man I ever knowed.'

'If that's so,' Meade said, as he reached for the reins of his horse, 'as Casson is range boss, why do you want me to go along?'

The chuckwagon was loaded ready to

leave. Standing near to the bunkhouse, Casson, powerfully built but running to fat, was issuing orders in his aggressive manner. The foreman hadn't taken to Henry Meade, making it plain that he regarded him as a gunslinger who was up to no good. This animosity hadn't bothered Meade up to now, and it wouldn't do so out on the range. What did worry him was leaving Letty behind with the Logans. Since getting to like Dan Logan and becoming really fond of the invalided Myrtle Logan, the girl's conscience had begun to trouble her. Meade would have liked to hang around to make sure that she didn't lose her nerve. Though it had been a close call for him in Tolula, the successful outcome made it seem like the gods had favoured the plan Letty and he were working to.

'Out on the range there's a thousand and one things for Charles to do. He's got twenty-four hands to watch over. Whoever it is must be working with Buck Woodward. I can't expect Charles to keep tabs on each of them day and night.'

'But that's what you want me to do?'

Dan Logan replied, 'I ain't got no right to ask you, son. But I don't want to see all I've worked for go under because of rustlers. You've got what it takes to sort this kind of thing out. You remind me a lot of myself in my younger days, though I didn't have your good looks. Let's put it this way, Meade: you help me out, bring this thieving to a halt, and I reckon I could see my way clear to doubling that reward you've got coming for finding my grandchild. Have we got a deal?'

'Maybe,' Meade answered coolly, as he mounted up.

But the thought of twice the reward went pleasantly over and over in his mind as he rode out with the others. Even so, his thinking was far from mercenary. Old Logan deserved not to be robbed of his cattle, and in helping the rancher Meade would be investing in Letty Dale's future.

As he rode he covertly studied the DL cowboys individually. They were a nondescript bunch, made into pseudo blood brothers by sharing twenty-four hours of every day with each other. There was one exception, the slim, taciturn Cass Gore, whose frosty green eyes held a dangerous light. Meade gathered that Gore was a newcomer to the outfit. Keeping himself aloof, Gore's affinity was obviously more with the six-gun he wore low and tied down, than it was with the other hands.

When three hours had passed under a burning sun, Casson rode up beside Meade to sarcastically enquire, 'I allow you can handle a right pretty gal, and you sure got yourself in well with the Logans, but do you know anything about working cattle, Meade?'

'I wouldn't be taking Dan Logan's money if I didn't, Casson.'

'Mr Logan may be paying your wages, but out here on the range I'm king. I gives the orders, you obey them,' Casson said, going on to issue a covert challenge. ‘Does that worry you, Meade?’

‘Not unless you cause it to, Casson.’

‘What if I do?’ a sneering Casson asked.

‘Then I guess it would cause you more worry than it will me.’

Casson ignored this, saying, ‘We’re going to start sweeping the range right now.’ Stretching out an arm he pointed. ‘See that flat mesa off to the east, Meade? That’s your marker. Over there, where Billy Wyndham’s setting up his chuckwagon, will be the centre of the camp. You hit the mesa then turn back and herd in all the cattle in your area. You got that?’

Meade nodded. Charles Casson’s contempt was showing through with the unnecessary explanation. Meade said flatly, ‘It isn’t too difficult to understand, Casson.’

‘Then make sure you get it right,’ Casson grunted before riding away.

Enjoying the solitude, Meade rode to the mesa at steady pace. It was edged with a rim-rock that stood some forty feet sheer above the flat lands. Riding among a tangle of cat-claw, mesquite and wild gourd vines, Meade knew Casson had deliberately picked this difficult section for him. Turning his horse he worked steadily. Seeking out cattle in arroyos and brush thickets, he headed west to eventually merge the animals he had gathered into the large, noisy, restless herd that had been assembled beside the camp.

An appetizing smell of cooking food reached him from the chuckwagon. Using one of three barrels of water set up for the purpose, he washed the trail dust from his face and body. The regular hands around him chatted and joked among themselves without once including him. When they squatted to devour salt pork, cornmeal and beans, washed down with green-berry coffee, they kept a distance between Meade and themselves. They seemed to believe it would diminish their standing to allow a stranger to enter the inner circle. Only Cass Gore, who was apparently not yet accepted, sat close to Meade as they ate. But Gore's silence meant that he was just a presence, not company.

With the meal over and darkness falling, Casson assigned night herders as the cattle fell silent and moved close together. An elderly, heavily whiskered man, produced a fiddle and began to play. The cowboys started off singing sentimental ballads, progressed to rollicking songs, then returned to sad choruses. Only Meade, Gore, and Casson didn't join in the singing, which trailed away into silence at a warning call from Casson.

From the meagre light of a sun bedding in a belt of blue-black clouds, Meade saw three mounted figures emerge like spectres from a dark veil of junipers. They rode steadily up to the fire, where the centre figure of the trio dismounted. Taking off a white stetson, the rider's head swung to release long black hair and settle it comfortably. A surprised Meade saw that it was a woman. Dramatically illuminated by the glow of the fire, her strong-featured face had a beauty that was stirringly primitive out here in the wilds. He heard a cowpuncher behind him identify her in a whisper to a buddy: Rosie Kirby.

'A bit late in the day for visiting, Miss Kirby,' Charles Casson greeted her as he stepped out of the shadows.

'Necessity makes time unimportant, Casson,' she responded in a voice that was low-pitched but carried far. 'How many head would you say you've lost?'

'Can't rightly say this early, Miss Kirby. We pulled in so many strays today that we'll be branding all day long tomorrow. Be another two or three days before I know if we've lost anything.'

'Oh, you'll have lost more than a few head, believe you me,' she said angrily. 'I've already lost more beef than I did in the whole of last year. It has to be stopped, Casson. It'll be months, if at all, before Sheriff Basso is back in the saddle, so it's up to us to make our own law. I'm going to see if we can't form some kind of cattleman's association around here like they have in other parts.'

Casson looked dubious. 'Dan Logan will be all for it, Miss Kirby, but I reckon as how you'll have a problem with Buck Woodward.'

'Then we'll go ahead without him,' a resolute Rosie Kirby announced.

Watching her scan the semi-circle formed by listening cowboys, Meade saw her gaze light on Cass Gore, who seemed to be taking no notice of what was going on. Obviously dismissing him, Rosie Kirby spotted Meade and walked slowly over to stand facing him.

Close up she was even more attractive. Maybe the poor light from the fire was fooling him, but her eyes were black and had a depth to them that held him spellbound. She pointed a short whip at him as if he was a horse she was about to buy in a sale.

'You must be Meade,' she said haughtily, 'the man they're all talking about in Tolula. Are you as good with a gun as they say you, are?'

Liking her looks but not her manner, Meade replied with a question of his own. 'I don't know; how good do they say I am?'

Annoyance briefly showed on her face, then she shook her head as if clearing that emotion away. Looking him straight in the eye, she said, 'Learn to show a bit of respect and you could work for me any time you like.'

Without another word and not waiting for him to reply, she turned to walk smartly away. Heading for where her horse and the two mounted men waited, she spoke to Casson without looking his way. 'Come across any Three Cs' stock, Casson, just send a man to let me know and I'll have them collected.'

'As you say, Miss Kirby,' Casson agreed.

Mounting up, she waved a hand to

no one in particular. Reining her horse about, she and her two companions disappeared into the night in the same mystical way they had arrived.

It puzzled Meade that there was no obvious reason for Rosie Kirby to have ridden into the DL camp. She had made a show of anger about continued rustling, but could have gained nothing by telling Charles Casson about it. Yet she wasn't the kind of woman to act without a purpose. What had been her purpose here? A thought came to him: maybe she and Casson were in on the rustling together, something which her alleged loss of stock would hide. This was so ridiculous that Meade rejected the notion.

The singing recommenced, but Rosie Kirby's visit, though brief, had shortened the evening. Just two ribald ditties were sung before the session ended with the singing of a sacred hymn. Soon afterwards, all the cowhands except the night herders were in their bedrolls.

Sleep eluded Henry Meade. Listening to the wailing of coyotes, some muted by distance, others close in, he thought of Letty Dale. Had the girl given way to her innate goodness and confessed that she was an imposter and he a trickster? In a strange way he would welcome it if she had. His well-planned scheme, finding out about the pewter lamp and staging Letty's bogus remembrance for Logan's benefit had lost a lot of its appeal. When the intended victims had been just names without faces, not real people, it had been easy.

Meade was reminding himself of how he wanted to start up in ranching again and that Letty and he had come too far to back out, when a furtive movement caught his attention.

Lying still, he looked carefully around. By the light of a moon that had climbed high to hang overhead like a great lantern, filling the camp area with a soft glow, he saw Cass Gore rise up out of his bedroll and move stealthily away, his saddle carried over one shoulder. Aware that Gore was heading for where the horses were held in a rope corral, Meade slid silently from his bedroll to pick up his saddle and follow at a distance.

Gore ducked under the loose rope. Whispering softly to calm the animals as he selected a horse, he dropped a bridle he was carrying over its head, and led it out. In deep shadow he saddled the horse. Biding his time until Gore walked the horse away into the night so as to make no noise, Meade quietly got himself a horse from the makeshift corral and saddled it.

A few hundred yards from the camp, Gore swung up into the saddle and set his horse off at a trot. Mounting up, Meade followed. It looked likely that he was about to end Dan Logan's problem for him. The behaviour of Cass Gore, the latecomer to the DL Ranch, was in keeping with an inside man working with a gang of rustlers.

After more than an hour spent riding

through the soft night air, Meade's suspicions were confirmed. He trailed Gore through a pass to where the terrain dropped away. From far down the slopes there came a low bawling. Then the thud of restless hoofs and the clicking clash of horns carried clearly through the night. Meade knew that a stolen herd was up ahead, and Cass Gore was heading for it.

As Meade cautiously neared a creek the ground became rocky. Up ahead he could see the blurred silhouette that was Gore dismount and lead his horse to keep the clipping sound of iron against rock to an absolute minimum. The cattle up ahead sounded uneasy, agitated. Any sudden noise in the night was likely to cause a stampede.

A camp-fire shone redly in the far distance. Aware that would be where Gore was making for, Meade was now prepared to let the slim man out of his sight. He would spy on Gore and whoever the rustlers were later. First he wanted to move among the stolen cattle in the hope of getting a glimpse of the brand or brands.

Spotting a little grove of cottonwood trees to his left, he avoided the rocky ground by heading in that direction across the grass. In among the trees he dismounted and was hitching the horse's reins to a branch when from close behind him came that unmistakable, metallic sound of the hammer of a six-gun being drawn back.

Caught dead to rights, Meade raised both hands to shoulder height and turned his upper body slowly. He found himself staring down the barrel of a six-gun held by a bearded man who had the haunted, hunted, dangerous look of a desperado. Taking his captor to be a rustler, Meade had this confirmed for him by the sight of two other men who stepped out from the criss-cross shadows cast by the moon through the trees. Both held rifles waist high, the muzzles covering him.

Meade had unsuspectingly ridden into a rustlers' outpost set up to protect the main party and the stolen herd. He must be losing his touch. To try drawing his Colt would be suicide, so he kept his arms raised as the two men with rifles moved up on him from behind. One plucked his gun from its holster while the other searched through his pockets, removing his few belongings which comprised mainly of the makings.

'Nothing here to say who he is, Matt,' the searcher reported to the man holding the revolver.

'Maybe he ain't the one, Matt,' the third desperado suggested, as he rammed Meade's gun down inside of his own belt.

A puzzled Meade wondered who they were expecting. It seemed that his fate depended on whether it was a friend or foe.

'Whoever he is he sure has no business hereabouts,' the man called Matt said in a grating voice that sounded like it had passed through a damaged throat. 'Tie his hands, Rufus.'

Meade's arms were roughly forced behind him and his wrists were tied with rope. As he put a knee in Meade's back to pull hard on the rope before tying it, one of the men, Meade figured it was Rufus, asked, 'We taking him in, Matt?'

'No point,' Matt replied. 'No need to go bothering the boss with some range bum. We'll just finish him off here.'

'We cain't risk a shot, Matt. It would send them critturs out there thunderin' off into kingdom come.'

'There'll be no shooting,' Matt said, as he walked over to stand in front of Meade. 'It'll give me a heap of pleasure to string him up from one of these here cottonwoods.'

Parting his tangled beard in what he probably imagined was a grin but was an ugly grimace that put broken discoloured teeth on display, he used both hands to pull down the turned-up collar of his coat. Fingers of one hand going inside of a filthy neckerchief, Matt pulled it down to reveal a rope burn that ran right round his neck. Purple in the moonlight, it had a pattern that was gouged deeply into the skin.

'That's what law-abiding folk did to Matt,' the third outlaw, speaking for the first time, informed Meade.

'Left me dangling there for dead,' Matt added in his painfully hoarse voice. 'But I am the son of a preacher-man, stranger, and the good Lord remembered the time I was regular in church as a boy. He spared me, stranger, do you hear me? The Lord spared me by sending along Rufus and Yate here, who cut me down just as I was drawing in my last breath.'

'That's what law-abiding folk do to rustlers,' Yate said solemnly.

'So seems like fair play that we do it to law-abiding folk,' Matt rasped.

'But we don't know for certain whether or not this is him, Matt.' Rufus seemed to be advising caution, Meade was pleased to note.

'Like I said, the fact that he came

sneaking in here's enough to say what he is,' Matt forcefully and gratingly overrode any objections. 'Fetch me a lariat, Yate.'

Yate moved away and Rufus crouched to lash Meade's ankles together. Up high in one of the cottonwoods a night bird uttered a mournful cry. The sound had a profoundly sad effect on an already dispirited Henry Meade. Yate was returning, carrying a coiled rope in one hand and leading Meade's horse with the other.

* * *

'We dug mesquite sprouts to burn for cooking and heating,' Myrtle Logan reminisced, recall of the bad old days bringing a tight little smile to her pale, withered-skinned face. 'It was worse than we had anticipated. On the way here we had stopped at farmhouses and been given milk, butter, eggs and bacon. When we arrived there was no one else but us apart from the Indians.

We didn't see them at the start, but we could hear a-whooping and a-hollering out there a-ways. I don't think your grandfather slept for more than half an hour at a time. He had only one pair of boots that were just torn, rusty lumps of leather. The soles of his feet were cut by stones and pierced by thorns and the like, but he never once considered giving up, never once did I hear him complain.'

Sitting comfortably in a rocking chair she guessed the old lady had used before being confined to bed, Letty was uneasy. Neither Myrtle nor Dan Logan made any enquiries about her past, both of them compensating for this by detailing the harrowing days and nights they had spent as early settlers. It hurt her to hear the ordeals they had endured. Before leaving to go on the round-up, Henry had pointed out how happy she had made the ageing pair. That was true, but Letty shrank more and more from the idea of taking over so easily the ranch that had cost Myrtle and Dan Logan so much. Yet though they were being deceitful, Henry Meade was desperate to return to being a rancher, and they were pleasing rather than harming the Logans.

'What was she . . . ?' Letty started to say unthinkingly, then quickly corrected herself 'What was I like as a baby?'

'Every bit as pretty as your mother was, every bit, and she was truly lovely, Letty.' The old woman stumbled over the name. 'I'll have to get accustomed to calling you Letty. To me you'll always be Ellen, but you can't be asked not to keep the name you've always known yourself as.'

'I've never known my mother's name,' Letty said, so caught up in the conversation that for a moment it was easy to fool herself that she was speaking the truth.

'Mary,' the old lady said wistfully. 'We buried her on that little hill yonder. I don't expect you noticed the place. I kept a little garden planted there through the years. I'm sure all the flowers are gone now.'

'No.' Close to tears, Letty shook her head. She had seen the colourful little plot on the hill, and had wondered. 'There are still flowers there, lots of them.'

A contented smile spread across the tired old face of Myrtle Logan. She sighed. 'I think that the Almighty is tending my little garden of remembrance for me.'

'I'm sure that He is,' Letty murmured. A lump in her throat threatened to choke her, and she changed the subject. 'What was my father like?'

'James Pilcher.' Myrtle Logan said the name musingly. 'Daniel doesn't like to hear his name spoken, but I feel the lad should be pitied rather than vilified. James didn't have the constitution for life out West, Letty. He was ill and failing for days before he ran off. I think that he had only two choices, either to become a coward or a corpse. James chose the former, as would any sane person.'

'Why is my grandfather so against him after all these years?'

'Because James left without saying goodbye,' Myrtle Logan replied, 'and because he would have been an extra gun, which may have been enough to save you and your mother when the Indians raided us.'

This tale of long ago was suddenly very real for Letty. The perceptive old lady saw that she was becoming upset, and said, 'I'm getting a little tired, Letty dear. You go down with your grandfather while I take a nap.'

Glad for an excuse to escape from a story that was torturing her conscience, Letty kissed the woman's wrinkled cheek and went out of the room. Voices came to meet her as she descended the wide staircase. She heard a woman's voice, attractively low-pitched, speak tersely.

'Five hundred head in one night, Dan. That's five hundred too damned many. Right now I'm working day and night running the Three Cs for the benefit of rustlers.'

'I'm right sorry to learn this, Rosie,' Letty heard Dan Logan say. 'I reckon Charles has found we've lost about the same.'

'He doesn't know if you've lost any beef yet, Dan. I rode to his camp to see him last night.'

'Then I'll prepare myself for bad news,' a glum Logan said.

More than halfway down the stairs, Letty stood still to listen as she heard the woman's voice speak Henry's name. 'That new man of yours, Dan, Meade, isn't it? I like the look of him. He could be useful to us both.'

'Meade's a good man to have on our side, Rosie. I've already asked him to keep an eye on things.'

'Good.'

The woman sounded pleased. Letty continued on her way down the stairs. Catching sight of the visitor, she was momentarily taken aback by her loveliness. Long, black, glossy hair framed a strong, high-cheek-boned face. The dark eyes that turned Letty's way as the woman heard her footfalls, were large and compelling.

'Ah, Letty,' a delighted Dan Logan exclaimed. 'Come, I would like you to meet a neighbour and dear friend, Rosie Kirby. Rosie, this is my granddaughter.'

Giving Letty a startlingly beautiful smile, Rosie Kirby said, 'I have to hand it to you, Dan Logan, you old son-of-a-gun. Nobody believed you, but you always said your grandchild would turn up one day.'

Rosie Kirby's words sent a terrible coldness right through Letty's body. They raised a possibility that neither Henry Meade nor she had considered for a moment. What if the real Logan granddaughter should show up?

Such a prospect was so shattering that Letty had to fight to regain control of herself before she could return Rosie Kirby's smile. When she did manage it, the expression froze painfully on her face.

4

There was a sombre silence as if the creatures of the night, and even the trees, were aware that something terrible was about to happen. They put Meade up onto his horse, with Yate standing by its head holding the reins, Rufus stood high in the fork of a tree, securing one end of a rope and dropping the noose down. Standing on a small hillock that put him on a level with the mounted Meade, Matt gave a satisfied chuckle as he reached up for the rope.

'This is my treat, boys,' the bearded man chortled as he fed the lasso over Meade's head and settled it round his neck. Then as if controlled by a switch, all amusement left Matt as he looked solemnly at Meade, who was surprised to see tears about to leak from the rustler's bloodshot eyes as he said, his voice more hoarse than ever, 'I pity ye, my friend. I know how you're feeling right now, exactly how you're feeling. It's something I never did get over, *mi amigo*. The memory fills my dark nights. Many's the time I've laid under a starry sky unable to sleep and blamed God for not letting them hang me.'

For a moment the emotion moving the bearded rustler came close to having Meade forget his own plight. But then whatever it was that had brought about a complete change of character in Matt, was gone. The rustler's beard parted to let a delighted laugh pass through as one of his men spoke up.

'This sidewinder ain't going to have no need to blame anyone, Matt,' Yate said. 'He's just about to become real dead.'

'Deader than Davy Crockett's cold ass,' Rufus agreed as he clambered down from the tree.

Though the rope was only resting lightly round his neck, Meade felt that it was already choking the life out of him. He knew it was fear fooling with his imagination. This wasn't the first time he had faced death, but previously it had been a gamble, a gratifying challenge as he and the man he faced waited to discover which of them was the fastest gun. Sitting on a horse, trussed like a turkey at Thanksgiving, was a whole lot different. Henry Meade had accepted that the kind of life he had lived since losing his ranch invited an early death, but this wasn't the way he would have chosen to go.

Now Dan Logan's reward would never be his. He wondered for a brief moment if Letty would be able to carry on the charade without him. He hoped so. It would make it easier to die if he was able to believe that one of the two of them would come out of the Logan plan a winner.

'I guess everything's just about fixed, boys,' Matt crowed as he jumped excitedly about, relishing what was to come. 'Let go of them reins, Yate. You give his bronc a whack, Rufus. Whatever your name is, my friend, may you go with God.'

From the corner of his eye, Meade saw Rufus raise an arm. Expecting the horse to lurch forwards, Meade tensed, waiting to feel the rope tighten around his neck. Never had he experienced such a dire feeling of helplessness. He tried to close his mind to the coming minutes, but failed miserably. The sounds made by the three men echoed hollowly as if he was already entering another world.

But Rufus didn't hit the horse. Instead, his arm froze halfway down as a voice spoke quietly but commandingly from out of the intense darkness created by the cottonwoods.

'Don't any one of you three make a move.'

Figures holding rifles, Meade counted six in all, came gliding slowly out of the shadows. Surrounded, the three rustlers stood docile in total surrender. Head down, Matt was muttering what sounded like a prayer but Meade guessed was a stream of angry cursing. The strange echoing of earlier ceased for Meade, and he heard the sounds of the night recommence as nature seemed to sense that the crisis was over.

But Matt suddenly sprang into action. With a roar of rage, he swung round to slap Meade's horse hard, shouting, 'Hang, God-dang ye, hang! They did it to me! They did it to me!'

The horse leapt forward with such force that Meade was dragged from the saddle by the rope around his neck. With the world falling away from underneath him, he felt himself dropping endlessly. Then the noose tightened and held, he was swinging in the air, gasping for breath. Vaguely, as if it was happening far off, he heard Matt's grunt of pain as the stock of a rifle crunched against his face, breaking the jawbone.

Dimly aware of this happening, Meade dangled from the tree, rapidly losing consciousness as his body rotated and swung. Once or twice he scraped painfully against the rough bark of the trunk, and then a red mist filled his head, shutting off his ears to the hushed, urgent voices speaking around him. The swirling red became a deep black, and he knew no more.

When he regained his senses, opening his eyes, welcoming the mellow light of the moon that soothed the raging pain that gripped the whole of his head, Meade found himself lying on the grass among the cottonwoods. Hunkering by his side, frowning worriedly down at him, was a man of about his own age. The man's stetson was pushed back, revealing curling brown hair that was cut short. The features of the tanned face were irregular, the eyelids heavy, the nose large, and the lips thickly prominent. Oversized white teeth were put on show in a relieved grin as the man noticed Meade looking around.

'Don't worry, pard, them three

rustlers been taken care of. I've strung up a few men in my time, but never one who kicked up so much fuss as that Matt guy.'

'I guess he just didn't want to die,' a voice from somewhere off to Meade's left said.

'You didn't make it no easier by smashing half his face in, Will,' another voice remarked. 'There weren't nothing to hold the rope that side. It kept slipping up over his head.'

They were unfeelingly discussing what must have been a terrible death. Remembering what the bearded rustler had said about a previous half-hanging, Meade could imagine how he would have struggled. God had granted Matt his fervent wish, and had ended his haunted nights. Meade fought the agony and dizziness in his head to sit up. The man beside him advised caution.

'Take it easy. You were just about a goner when Reggie cut you down.'

The man had gestured to a tall, rangy

cowhand standing in a half-circle of five men. Meade gave him a nod of thanks, causing himself an increase in pain in the process.

'I'm Buck Woodward,' the man sitting on his heels beside Meade introduced himself. 'I own the Running M outfit.'

Though the pain was abating, learning that this was Woodward made Meade's spirits drop. With the rustled herd not far off, it looked as if Dan Logan was right about his neighbour. Meade resigned himself to having exchanged three captors for six. They had cut him down, but it seemed he was still a prisoner, and there was nothing to stop them putting another rope round his neck.

'I'm Henry Meade,' he said.

'I guessed that much,' Woodward nodded, his hound-like face expressionless. 'You're the talk of Tolula and all points north, south, east and west, pard. Seems like you handled yourself real well in town, Meade, but you didn't do so good with those three *hombres*.'

'I was . . . ' Meade began, about to say that he had been following Cass Gore, but stopped on realizing that Gore must have been riding to rendezvous with Woodward at the rustled herd. What didn't make sense was Buck Woodward rescuing him and hanging three of his own men. Could be that he had some use for Meade, and had callously carried out the hangings to separate himself from the rustling.

'We know who you were following,' Woodward cryptically informed him.

Getting to his feet, Meade was hit by a wave of giddiness and nausea. As he swayed, Woodward reached out a hand in an attempt at steadying him. Meade avoided the rancher's grasp. He never took help from anyone.

'I suppose there's going to be another necktie party right now,' Meade said, finding speaking an effort. His throat felt badly swollen inside, and was sore.

First registering shock, Woodward's heavy featured face altered into an expression of mirth. 'Looks to me that rope round your neck kinda tangled your thinking, Meade. Would we cut you down just to string you up again? I'm a rancher, pard, not a cattle thief.'

'There's a rustled herd not far off,' Meade pointed out, gesturing with his head in the direction of where the stolen cattle were held.

'I ain't about to argue with you about that, pard. That's what we were watching when we found you was in trouble,' Woodward nodded, adding, 'The men holding them dogies are just renegade trash like the three who grabbed you, pard. There ain't no sense in nailing them. We were watching and waiting to find out who's behind all this rustling.'

'That makes sense I guess,' a still unconvinced Meade acknowledged, 'but the way I heard it is that you haven't lost any beef.'

'Trouble is, Meade, you've been

listening to Dan Logan's nonsense,' Woodward rebuked him. 'The old fella don't have a good word to say about me. It's right that I haven't lost any stock to rustlers. There has to be a reason for that, but I ain't yet fathomed it. But I'm mighty fond of Rosie Kirby, so I don't take kindly to her being robbed. And, believe it or not, I'm a right neighbourly person and I don't like Dan Logan losing beef, even though he thinks it's me who's responsible.'

This sounded reasonable, and Meade was ready to accept it, at least for the time being. Woodward passed him his six-gun that they had retrieved from Matt and his two men. Checking that the bullets hadn't been removed from the chamber, Meade let the gun drop into its holster. Looking Woodward in the eye he asked, 'What now?'

With a shrug, Woodward replied, 'That's up to you, pard. You're a free man, so I guess you can ride whatever whichway the wind don't blow in your face. But I reckon that you have to give thought to that girl you rode in with. That being so, most probably you'll want to stay on at the DL.'

'Yep, that's what I intend doing,' Meade confirmed. He enquired challengingly, 'You got any objection to that, Woodward?'

'Like I said, pard, you can do whatever you feel like doing.' Buck Woodward studied the sky and a gradually fading moon. 'Seems like you got time before sun-up to get back to camp and crawl into your bedroll so's you'll never be missed. Watch out for that Charles Casson, pard. He can be a real mean cuss.'

Not answering, Meade saw that his horse was being led towards him, obviously on instructions from Woodward. The five cowboys stood close, not menacingly but obviously ready to do Woodward's bidding. Meade's nausea and giddiness had completely subsided, and the only reminder of his brush with death was now a soreness around his neck. Relieved that he wasn't regarded as a prisoner, he was ready to mount up and ride off, but the rancher raised a hand to stay him.

'You was messing with things that don't concern you tonight, Meade. It's best you don't do that.'

'To me that sounds like a warning, Woodward,' Meade said flatly, as he swung up into the saddle.

'Then I reckon that you'd best take it the way it sounds, pard.'

Reaching for the reins, Meade looked down on the rancher. 'I owe you my life, Woodward. I'm real grateful.'

'We just happened along at the right time,' Buck Woodward said with a big-toothed smile. 'Like I said, you're playing a dangerous game. You ain't the type to accept a warning, pard, but I reckon as how you'll do something for me.'

'You just have to do the asking, Woodward,' Meade assured him. Whatever crooked game Woodward was playing didn't alter the fact that Meade was in debt to him.

'All I want is for you not to mention to anyone that you saw me out here tonight, pard.'

This peculiar request was evidence enough for Meade. If the rancher's business out here in the night involved taking care of his neighbours' cattle, then he had nothing to hide. Yet Woodward was obviously badly worried right now.

Not replying, Meade was moving his horse away when Woodward called after him,

'Do I have your word on that, Meade?'

Slowing his horse, Meade, without turning his head, gave the only answer that the circumstances allowed him. 'You have my word.'

* * *

'It's a pity Meade didn't come into town with you, Miss Dale. I'd sure liked to have thanked him, too.'

Moses Basso showed no visible signs of having been shot and wounded. But Letty guessed from the stiff way he moved that his body was heavily bandaged. As hard as the iron bars of his combined office and jailhouse, the sheriff had an open air of total honesty and Letty instantly took to him. She had ridden into Tolula with Dan Logan that Thursday afternoon to find an insistent Ikey Kindler saying that he'd had a firm order from Basso that he wanted to see her and Dan.

'Meade's on the round-up with Charles, Moses,' Dan Logan informed the sheriff.

The sheriff gave a pleased nod. 'A good man to have on your side, by all accounts, Dan, but . . . '

'But what, Moses? Spit it out.'

Worn chair creaking as he reached for a whiskey bottle, Basso produced two glasses after he had raised his eyebrows questioningly at Letty, who shook her head in refusal. Pouring two drinks, the sheriff looked up at Dan Logan.

'Des Harker ain't complaining. Meade brought him more business in one day than he's had all year. Had to send out for more wood to finish the coffins,' Basso said with a wry smile. 'But the word is that Meade can be real trouble if he's against you. You sure you know what you're doing having this Henry Meade out at the DL, Dan?'

'I ain't got no doubts,' Dan Logan replied. 'He brought Letty to me, and I can't fault him. Sure, I can tell a hard man when I see one, but I ain't too old to handle anyone who cuts up rough with me.'

'I'll accept that in general, Dan, but from his reputation it's possible that neither you nor me have ever been a match for Henry Meade.'

Letty could accept what the sheriff was saying, but only in part. You didn't have to be around Henry Meade long to sense that, quiet though he was in manner, he wasn't a man to cross. What she couldn't subscribe to was that he was in any way a danger to Dan Logan.

'Don't reckon as how it will ever come to a showdown between Meade and me,' Logan said. 'I trust him enough to have him watch over things on the round-up, but I don't want Charles to think I've put Meade over him.'

'Casson being the ornery cuss that he is, he's probably already madder'n a gopher without a hole,' the sheriff grinned; then went quiet in thought before saying, 'One way you could put this right, Dan, without treading on your ramrod's toes, is to have me swear Henry Meade in as a deputy. That way he could take care of your interests kinda independent-like.'

The suggestion pleased Dan Logan. 'That's a mighty fine idea, Moses, if Meade will go for it.'

'We'll find out if you get him to ride into town to see me.'

'I'll do that, Moses,' Logan said, slapping his thigh in excitement. 'Yep, I sure will. I'll feel a heap better with Meade around, specially if he's got a badge to back him up.'

'I should be out there, too,' a frustrated Basso said.

'You forget the range and rest up awhile, Moses,' Dan Logan advised. 'You overlook the fact that you ain't a young man no more.'

'Now that's really something coming from a crumple-skinned old longhorn like yourself, Dan Logan,' the sheriff chuckled, before asking, his face serious, 'Have you lost many head this fall?'

Though the friendly banter created a pleasant atmosphere, Letty was impatient to get away and back to the ranch house. Ikey Kindler had a huge and magnificent painting with a beautiful gold frame waiting for Dan Logan when they had reached town. It was a scene inside of a Paris club, full of life and colour, and she knew how Myrtle Logan would love it. Letty just couldn't wait to see the delight on the careworn face of the lovely old lady when Dan

Logan presented her with the picture.

'Charles ain't yet had time to figure if any stock's missing, Moses,' Logan was saying as Letty slowed her day-dreaming about the painting. 'But Rosie Kirby came to tell me the Three Cs had some heavy losses. I've asked Henry Meade to have a scout around out there. What we need, when you're back in the saddle, Moses, is enough evidence for us all to move in on Buck Woodward.'

Looking at Letty, Basso released a long, exasperated sigh. 'There you go again, Dan. You're as obstinate as a prospector's jackass. Not only isn't there anything to point to Woodward as leader of the rustlers, but everything I've seen says that he isn't.'

'That shiny star pinned to your breast means that you have to say these loco things, Moses,' an irritated Dan Logan protested. 'But Rosie Kirby and me are mad enough about being robbed to make our own law. Iffen you won't help us, then we'll get them rustlers ourselves.'

'I'll help you catch the rustlers, *the rustlers*, but not get Buck Woodward.'

'Same blasted thing,' Dan Logan snorted.

'Dan, you'll be the death of me,' the sheriff said with an exaggerated groan. 'Look, if Meade plays it our way, just leave the law to me and him. You've found your granddaughter, and a right pretty girl she is, a real compliment to you. Why not take care of Myrtle and enjoy life with Letty?'

'I ain't got a lot of life left, Moses,' Dan Logan gritted between clenched teeth. 'It's Letty I'm thinking of. If I stop this cattle-thieving now, then she'll be set up for life with the DL. If it goes on, then there'll be nothing for me to hand down to her.'

Letty thrilled at hearing this. The old man had fully accepted her as his kin. Soon she was going to be the somebody she'd always promised herself she'd become. Once again she was aware of Sheriff Basso studying her, covertly but intently. He'd been doing this most of the time she'd been in his office. It wasn't the kind of lecherous ogling she'd had to endure most of her life, and while working for Nelly in particular. Though she wouldn't have expected that sort of thing from Basso, it wouldn't have worried her like his clearly professional scrutiny.

'You take chances on this, Dan,' the sheriff cautioned, 'and you might not be around to hand anything over to your granddaughter. Let Charles Casson, and Henry Meade if you like, take care of the rustlers, while you keep back so far that you don't even get a whiff of gunsmoke.'

'That ain't my way and you knows that, Moses Basso,' Dan Logan said testily as he got his his feet, ready to leave. Letty stood up with him.

'It's about time you made it your way,' Sheriff Basso commented as he walked to open the door for them.

As Dan Logan and Letty were passing the sheriff on their way out,

Basso frowned as he looked into Letty's face.

'I'm pretty sure, Miss Dale,' the sheriff began speculatively, 'that I know you from somewhere.'

Blood running cold, wanting to flee from Basso's searching eyes, Letty stammered, hopefully. 'I waited table at the Portage Hotel down in Raimondo, Sheriff. Maybe that's where you saw me.'

Basso disappointed Letty by giving a negative shake of his head. It unnerved her to perceive that Sheriff Basso wasn't just curious, he was downright suspicious of her. 'No, that can't be it, Miss Dale. The last time I was in Raimondo was likely afore you were born.'

'That's a sign of getting old, Moses, having your memory play tricks,' Logan teased the sheriff. 'I'll allow you, like me, never laid eyes on Letty till she rode into Tolula.'

'My memory's never let me down, Dan. I'll remember. I never forget a face.'

Make this the first time, Letty pleaded inside of her head as she and Dan Logan took their leave of Basso. Please forget my face, Sheriff!

But she knew that Moses Basso wouldn't do what she hoped and prayed he would do. A lawman through and through, he would gnaw at the problem of where he had seen her until he found the answer. Climbing up onto the buckboard, she uttered up a silent prayer that if Basso had seen her in the past, it would be in a situation that wouldn't affect her and Henry Meade's plan.

Somewhere deep inside she knew that this wouldn't be so.

5

The small herd of cattle they had collected from out of the brush were immobile due to tiredness. Meade and Cass Gore crouched beside the coldly refreshing waters of a creek. Getting back to the camp unnoticed in the night, Meade had discovered Gore already there in his bedroll. Gore was involved in the rustling somehow, and Meade wanted to question the slim, mysterious man. He had welcomed Charles Casson's decision to send him and Gore out together that morning, but up to now Meade's taciturn, temporary partner had not uttered one word. Meade was determined to take full advantage of the opportunity now on offer. Slaking his thirst, he soaked his bandanna to wash his face, then squeezed the water from the neckerchief and stood up.

Still hunkering, Gore was as distant and detached as ever. He appeared not even to know that Meade was standing above him. About to ask a question concerning Gore's actions during the previous night, Meade was taken suddenly and totally by surprise.

One minute the lightly built man was sitting on his heels, the next he exploded into action. Coming up fast and positioning himself all in the same movement, he shot out a right-hand punch that caught Meade full on the jaw. It was an amazingly heavy blow from so slender a man. Lifted off his feet by it, Meade landed hard on his back.

For a split second he was paralysed and unable to draw in a much-needed breath. But control of his body returned, accompanied by a flaring rage. Intending to get up and retaliate, Meade found he was too late. Gore stood over him, placing his right foot hard on Meade's throat. The pressure was choking Meade, and the high heel of Gore's boot gouged cruelly into the side of his neck. The pain of this was worsened by the heel digging into the rope burns remaining from the aborted hanging.

Twisting his foot to increase the effect, Gore spoke abstractly, like a man discussing routine work. 'You made a big mistake trailing me last night, Meade. This is a warning. Don't ever meddle in my business again.'

Gore seemed to be waiting for some kind of assent. But Meade, with his throat out of action, was unable to speak. It got worse for him as Gore put more weight on his foot.

'Keep out of it, Meade, or you're a dead man.'

With that, Gore stepped away, leaving Meade choking and gagging for breath. Coming up on to one elbow, holding his agonized throat as he coughed and spluttered, Meade watched Gore walk slowly and nonchalantly away from him. Still barely able to drag in anything like enough air to fill his lungs, anger lent Meade the strength to scramble to his feet and charge at the departing Gore.

Hearing him come, Gore pivoted on one heel. As supple as a rattlesnake, he weaved his upper body to one side so that Meade's bunched right fist missed his head. But it did slam against the lighter man's shoulder, spinning him off balance so that Meade, fast recovering, was able to land a stinging punch to Gore's face, the knuckles splitting the skin along the length of Gore's prominent cheekbone.

Blood flowing from his face, Gore slipped a follow-up punch from Meade over his shoulder. Then with astonishing speed, he used right and left-hand punches to beat a tattoo on Meade's ribs. They were bruising punches and Meade used his elbows to protect his body. Quick as a flash, Gore switched tactics to rip punches into Meade's face. With cuts above both eyes, and his nose streaming blood, Meade was forced to give ground, but Gore came with him, relentlessly slamming a barrage of punches home.

Already weakened by the battering he was being subjected to, Meade knew that he had to think his way out, devise a plan of action, otherwise he would be beaten to a pulp. Never had he met a man with the speed of Cass Gore.

Spitting blood as Gore's knuckles split his top lip open against his teeth, Meade dropped down on one knee as if too badly hurt to remain standing. Deprived of a target for his fists, Gore drove his right knee forwards, aiming for Meade's bloodied face. Shifting slightly, Meade grabbed Gore's leg and pulled. In the way Meade had planned, the smaller man lost his balance. As Gore fell, Meade twisted the leg so that his opponent landed face down. Keeping hold of the leg, Meade wrapped his own left leg in behind Gore's knee, intending to bring all his weight to bear so as to snap the ligaments in Gore's leg, crippling him.

But Gore was an accomplished

fighter. As Meade was bringing his body down, Gore lashed out with his other foot. The sole of the boot cracked against Meade's right temple, stunning him, sending him flying backwards.

Up on his feet in an instant, Gore moved in ready to stomp on the prone Meade. But Meade rolled as Gore jumped high. Feet together, Gore came down, but his boots crashed harmlessly to the ground beside Meade. Coming up onto his feet, throwing punches as he came, Meade rocked Gore with a left and right to the head, but the lighter man kept his feet and countered. Punches were ripping into Meade again, who realized that though he could hit harder, he could never match Gore for speed.

A blow to the chin forced Meade to take a few backward steps. Colliding with his horse, he sent it skittishly crashing into Gore's mount, and the two animals began shrieking and threshing around in panic.

Propelled forwards when the horses

bumped hard against him, Meade caught Gore a heavy blow to the side of the head. Shaken for the first time in the fight, Gore dropped to one knee. Believing he had gained the advantage, Meade was poised to move in for the finish. But the tough Gore was already coming up, ready to meet and handle any attack.

But luck came to help Meade in the form of a flailing hoof of a horse. Gore was in a crouch from which he could either defend or launch an attack, when Meade's horse reared. With a dull thud the hoof hit the back of Gore's head, instantly felling him.

Meade momentarily hesitated, but a reminder of what a formidable opponent he faced came as, unbelievably, Gore came up on to his hands and knees. With the horses still creating pandemonium, Meade knew that he didn't have a choice. A groggy Gore was kneeling now, and Meade realized that within a few minutes the desperate fight was likely to recommence. Aware that he had to finish it, he stepped in to grab Gore by the shirt-front. Pulling the man to his feet, Meade held him with one hand and hit him with the other.

With Gore reeling helplessly, Meade used both hands to beat him senseless, not ceasing his relentless attack until Gore fell to the ground and lay still.

Pulling a wide leaf from a bush, Meade wiped the blood from his knuckles. Then he calmed both horses, hitching Gore's securely. Meade wouldn't leave a man out there without a horse, and he knelt beside the unconscious Gore to satisfy himself that the man would eventually recover and be able to make his way back to camp.

Only then did Meade mount up, skilfully moving his horse this way and that to get the group of cattle moving off in the direction of the camp.

It was dusk when he got there, turning his cows in with the main bunch for the night herders to take care of. No one seemed to notice the absence of Cass Gore, and the dimness of twilight hid Meade's battered features from them. He was at the chuck-wagon, holding his plate as Billy Wyndham shovelled baked beans on it, when Charles Casson came up to him. The foreman took a long time in scrutinizing Meade's cut and bruised face before he asked a question.

'Will Gore be coming back?'

Taking a sip of coffee from his mug, Meade answered with a shrug.

'Well now,' a falsely amiable Casson said, 'it don't never matter to me what you loco mavericks get up to out there in the brush. That's as long as it don't interfere with the work, you understand. The way I see it, you've lost me a hand, so it seems pretty right that you do two men's work until, and if, Cass Gore gets back.'

'That won't bother me, Casson.'

'It don't bother me none, neither, Meade,' Casson said. 'Thing is, though, you ain't going to be here for me to work your butt off. Mr Logan wants you to head back to the ranch at first light.'

Casson seemed far more disgruntled by Dan Logan calling Meade in, than he did by the loss of Gore. He walked away, leaving Meade puzzled. The only reason he could come up with for Logan wanting to see him, was that the old man had learned that he was being duped by Letty and himself.

If that was the case, then all Meade could do was to ride on and seek to regain his fortune elsewhere. Having brought Letty here he would have to take her with him. He'd see that she was fixed up somewhere safe and comfortable before leaving her.

Meade ate his meal alone, as usual, and stayed apart from the others throughout the ritual sing-song. Bedding down for the night, he took the precaution of slipping his gun from its holster and keeping it close at hand under the blankets. Always a light sleeper, coming alert within a split second if a situation called for it, he did little more than doze that night.

But Cass Gore didn't return during the hours of darkness. Neither was he back at sun-up when Meade was standing by the chuckwagon eating a hurried breakfast. This was where Charles Casson spotted him and walked over.

'What happened out on the range yesterday, Meade?'

'Ask Gore,' Meade responded gruffly, carrying on eating his breakfast.

'Now that gives me a bit of a problem,' Casson complained, 'seeing as how Gore ain't yet turned up. You finish that grub off right quick, Meade, and head back for the ranch. When you gets there, give Mr Logan a message from me. You tell him that we've lost more head this year than we ever have at any fall round-up. I ain't had chance for no proper count, but you can tell him for sure that one helluva lot of beef has gone missing.'

Nodding to say that he had got the message, Meade drained the last drop of coffee from his mug and walked to where he had left his horse after saddling it. Casson called to him.

'And Meade.'

Pausing, Meade turned to face the ramrod. 'What?'

'If Gore ain't here when you get back, then you'll have me to answer to. If this rustling ain't stopped pronto, then we're all going to be out of work. I need all the men I can. You be sure to tell Mr Logan that.'

'I'll tell him,' Meade replied as he mounted up.

* * *

Not until she saw the approaching riders did Letty Dale confess to herself that she had been foolish to stray so far from the ranch. She had felt confident after having insisted on taking the buckskin for a morning ride. When a buckskin is mean it is very mean, and this one had the speed and spirit to get her away from any danger, but that was before the animal had gone lame for some reason. All she could do now was stand beside the horse and await her fate. If the trio riding up on her were ruffians, then she was at their mercy out here. Being so headstrong was her major fault, she knew that. First, she had openly defied Dan Logan on the issue of the buckskin, then she had secretly disobeyed him by riding well beyond the limits the old man had set for her. Letty had been motivated by the hope that she would meet Henry Meade riding in. That was stupid of her, too, because she couldn't be sure from which direction he would come.

'Good morning, ma'am.'

The lead rider had taken off his stetson with a flourish. Politeness was a reassuring sign, Letty told herself. He had short, curly hair topping a face made solemn by its lack of symmetry. The big-toothed smile he afforded her was friendly.

'Good morning,' she replied stiffly. For all his ruggedness he didn't appear to be a threat to her, and his two companions were plainly subordinates who wouldn't do anything not sanctioned by him.

Dismounting, he walked over to where she stood. Moving round the buckskin, lifting one of its legs at a time to examine the hoof before letting it fall. Straightening up, he looked at with an expression of mingled unhappiness and sympathy.

'It strikes me, miss, that wherever you've ridden out from you've got a long walk back,' he drawled. 'This buckskin of your'n won't be fit to ride for a week or more. If you've no objection to riding up behind me, I'd be happy to take you back home, miss. Where would that be?'

'The DL Ranch,' a relieved Letty replied.

The man laughed, a short but rumbling laugh that came from deep in his barrel chest. 'Excuse me, miss, but that's sure enough amusing from where I'm standing. Would I be right in thinking that you're the long-lost granddaughter of Dan Logan?'

'Yes, I'm Letty Dale,' Letty acknowledged sharply, wondering what he found to be so funny.

'Maybe you'll understand and forgive me, miss,' he said, his face solemn once more, 'when I say that I'm Buck Woodward. I guess you've heard of me.'

'I've heard of you, Mr Woodward.'

'I don't doubt it, I don't doubt it.' Woodward pursed his thick lips in consternation. 'You wouldn't be at Logan's place more'n five minutes before you learned all about me. So, Miss Dale, I suppose you see me as the enemy?'

Buck Woodward wasn't the man Letty had been led to expect. Studying him, she found herself liking what she saw. Though he had the rough edges of a man shaped by a harsh environment, gentlemanly qualities showed through. He certainly wasn't the ogre Dan Logan made him out to be, and she just couldn't envisage him as a rustler.

'I have no reason to regard you as an enemy, Mr Woodward,' she said.

'Well said,' he smiled at her. 'I guess I'd choose my words with care if I was stuck out here on the range with a lame horse.'

'My circumstances have nothing to do with it, Mr Woodward,' Letty told him firmly. 'Had I reason to regard you in a poor light, which I haven't, then I would have no hesitation in doing so, even if it meant my going fifty miles on foot.'

Looking at her intently, face serious, he remained silent. Then his big white teeth showed in a pleased smile as he complimented her. 'Shucks, miss, I allow that you're speaking the truth, and I admire you for it.' Leaning low out of the saddle, he extended his arm, saying, 'Grab hold with both hands, miss, and I'll pull you up.'

Embarrassed but having no alternative but to accept, Letty caught hold of the proffered arm. Through the material of Woodward's coat she felt his muscles tense and bulge as he effortlessly lifted her from the ground and swung her up behind him on to the horse.

* * *

Henry Meade was a man who liked each day to run close to the way he thought it would on opening his eyes in the morning. It was late afternoon now, and this particular day hadn't run true to any of his expectations. At the DL ranch house he'd found Dan Logan beside himself with worry over Letty, who was long overdue from a morning ride. That made it difficult for the old man to concentrate on what he had to tell Meade, and worry over the girl caused Meade difficulty in taking in what was expected of him. He had agreed to become Moses Basso's deputy, but had wanted to delay going into town to see the sheriff until he'd ridden out to find Letty and bring her back safely.

'No, I'll send Haughty out.' Old man Logan had insisted on having his half-crippled ex-wrangler go after the girl. 'You brought Casson's message in, Meade, so you know how bad things are. Basso's expecting you, so the sooner you get into town and back, the sooner we'll put a stop to this thieving.'

Meade had doubts about that then, and they were still with him. Whoever was responsible for the large-scale rustling was both powerful and clever. Having a deputy's badge pinned on the chest of one man wouldn't be enough to solve the problem. But he had bowed to the old man's wishes because it would give him the chance to find out what role Buck Woodward was playing in it all. Also, if Cass Gore should show up, Meade wanted to find out just how he was involved. This time he would take the sensible course of relying on his gun rather than his fists. It was possible that the enigmatic Gore had the edge on him that way, too. There was only one way to find out.

The essential thing for his future was to keep on the right side of Dan Logan, he told himself now as he rode slowly into Tolula. It was late afternoon and the town had a peaceful look in contrast to when he had last been there. Recognizing Kindler's store, where Letty and he had first contacted Dan Logan, he looked for the sheriff's office. It stood at the first corner of the next block, and he gently urged his horse towards it.

He got an uncertain but friendly smile from a young girl with hair that matched the sun. Two cowboys wearing cartridge belts and revolvers, lounged outside of the Faro Wheel, waiting for the doors to open. As Meade rode past they eyed him with the suspicion of men who live in a hostile environment. Meade gave them a nod, but neither of them returned his silent greeting. With a flick of his eyes he checked their horses at the rail. Both had a Three Cs brand. They were Rosie Kirby's men.

Dismounting at the sheriff's office,

Meade removed his stetson and used it to beat the dust off his clothing. Trying to recall what Sheriff Basso looked like, having only caught a glimpse of him during the hectic activity of the shoot-out, he went in. Standing up from the chair behind the desk was an old man who had been robbed of his teeth and the ability to stand straight by advancing age.

'What can I do for you, mister?'

'I'm here to see Sheriff Basso,' Meade answered.

The old fellow squinted and frowned as if Meade had come to the wrong place, in the wrong town, looking for the wrong sheriff. Then he identified himself. 'I'm Jasper Nailham. Whatever your business is, mister, you can talk to me. I take care of things here while Moses is away.'

'It has to be the sheriff, Jasper,' Meade said, friendly-like but able to see that the old man was hurt.

'Suit yourself,' Nailham grunted. 'But Moses is out of town. Gone down

Coldflint way to see the sawbones who's a'fixing his wound. Won't be back before morning.'

'Then I'll stay in town overnight,' Meade, disappointed, informed the old man. This wasn't what he wanted to do. Desperately worried about Letty, he'd hoped to settle his business with the sheriff quickly, and return to the DL without delay.

'You'll get yourself a decent enough bed down at Lank Ducking's hotel,' Jasper advised.

The hotel was small but comfortable, and reminiscent of the place in Raimondo where his first meeting with Letty Dale had taken place. A Mexican boy waited on the tables, and Meade, discovering that he was ravenously hungry, ordered a thick, juicy beefsteak with plenty of spuds.

While he was waiting for the food to be brought to him, he saw Rosie Kirby step inside the door. Taking off her broad-brimmed hat, she shook her long black hair loose as Meade had seen her do out on the range. Head held high and proud, she scanned the place. Spotting Meade, she walked over to stand beside his table, giving a little despairing shake of her head as she looked down on him. He stood up.

'Very chivalrous,' she acknowledged with a faint smile, taking a chair across the table from him. Meade regained his seat as she continued, 'Most men out here don't have your manners, Henry Meade, but I still don't know what I'm going to do with you. You've cost me money and come close to ruining my plans.'

Meade stared silently at her. The wild attractiveness of her face as he remembered it on the range was softened and shaded into a stunning beauty by mellow lighting from the dining-room lamps. The sight of her made it difficult for him to find his voice.

'Forgive me, Miss Kirby,' he managed to say at last, 'but I don't understand what you're saying.'

'What I'm saying, Henry Meade, is

that you beat Cass Gore half to death,' she said, meeting his gaze and holding it.

Bewildered, Meade protested, 'Cass Gore works for the DL, for Dan Logan.'

'Maybe it looks that way,' Rosie Kirby half-agreed, 'but Cass Gore is a range detective engaged by me.'

6

'Stop right where you are, or, by jiminy, I'll blast you right off the back of that horse.'

Woodward and Letty had come on alone after he had sent his two hands back to the Running M. They reached the DL with the limping buckskin trailing behind them. Since they had neared the ranch house Letty had feared something like this would happen. She peered fearfully round one of the wide shoulders of Buck Woodward, to see a furious Dan Logan with a rifle held to his shoulder pointing straight at Woodward. Logan was squinting along the sights, a wild look in the eye he had open, and his mouth moving as if rehearsing his next shouted warning.

'Hold on there, Logan,' Woodward called. 'I ain't Sitting Bull at the head of a war party. I'm your neighbour.'

'I know well who and what you are, Woodward, a thieving varmint. I hadn't lost so much as one steer until you came about here.'

Hearing the argumentative exchange, the Chinese cook, who had been at the well, hurried back to the house in his bent over, flat-footed way. Eager not to be a victim of the violence likely to break out, he carried back a bucket as empty as it had been when he'd left the house.

'There's no call to get all riled up, old-timer,' Woodward attempted to pacify Logan. 'I've brought your grand-daughter back home.'

Letty leaned out a little further, making herself part of the target knowing that Dan Logan wouldn't risk a shot if there was a chance of hurting her. She and Buck Woodward had spoken little on the way back, but there had been a rapport between them that made the ride over gently rolling grazing land enjoyable. But now as a purple haze softened and made the outlines of the buildings obscure in what should be a tranquil dusk, the reception her rescuer was receiving from Dan Logan made her ashamed.

Reaching an arm round behind him for Letty to catch hold of, Woodward lowered her carefully to the ground. Thanking him, Letty ran to Dan Logan, reaching out to the rifle that he still held trained on Woodward. The old rancher stepped away from her, keeping the rifle aimed. His lined face was white with anger.

'Keep back, girl,' he asked, rather than ordered Letty, before calling to Woodward, 'Get off my land, Woodward. I'll count to three.'

'But Mr Woodward helped me,' Letty pleaded. 'I'd still be out there now if it wasn't for him.'

Her entreaty fell on deaf ears. Dan Logan began his count. 'One!'

'This don't make sense. There is no reason why we should be enemies,'

Woodward attempted to make the peace.

'There's thousands of reasons — the thousands of head of stock I've lost since you been here, Woodward,' the elderly rancher shouted. 'Two!'

With Woodward showing no sign of leaving, Letty called to him. 'Please, Mr Woodward. It's for the best if you leave.'

'Nobody holds a gun on me and tells me what to do, Miss Dale,' Woodward said flatly.

'*Three!*'

Realizing that Dan Logan was serious with his shouted count, Letty launched herself at him just as he pulled the trigger. The explosion of the rifle being fired deafened her for a moment. Ears ringing, she took a frightened look in Woodward's direction. He was still in the saddle, but his stetson was lying in the dust just behind his horse. Going icily cold from head to toe, Letty grasped that the bullet from the rifle had knocked the hat off. Had she not intervened it would have blown out Buck Woodward's brains.

Watching Woodward coolly dismount and bend to retrieve his hat, Letty clung on to Dan Logan lest he bring up the rifle again. She could feel him trembling, but wasn't sure whether it was from rage or shock from having come so close to killing Buck Woodward.

'You're a danged fool, Dan Logan,' Woodward said, as he calmly examined a bullet hole in his stetson before putting it back on his head and climbing up into the saddle. Reining his horse around, he said, 'I'm leaving now, Miss Dale. You can let go of him.'

In a quandary, Letty, afraid that if she released the old rancher he would fire another shot at Woodward, clung on.

'Release me, child,' Logan told her.

Woodward's back was to them now as he prepared to ride away. Reluctantly, Letty took her arms from around Dan Logan, alarmed when he lifted the rifle and shouted to Woodward, 'The next time we come face to face,

Woodward, there'll be gunplay.'

'What point would there be to that?' Woodward enquired, turning his horse back so that he was facing them.

'It'll stop the cattle thieving,' Logan said. 'I don't intend to let years of hard work go to waste, Woodward. This ranch will be my granddaughter's soon, and I mean to see that it's worth having.'

For a moment it seemed that Woodward was going to say something. But he changed his mind, shook his head, raised a hand to Letty, and swung his horse round. As she watched Woodward push his horse into a trot, she turned to Logan.

'You could have killed him.'

'I *should* have killed him, Letty,' Dan Logan chillingly corrected her.

In that same gradually falling dusk, Henry Meade walked a wooden sidewalk in Tolula. Lines of horses with the Running M brand were hitched to the rails outside of the Faro Wheel. The sound of a clanking piano that had been catchily melodic when filtering out into the street, became ear-jarringly tuneless as Meade entered the crowded saloon. He had to force his way through half-drunken cowboys to reach the bar. From snatches of conversation that rose above the general roar, Meade gathered that the Running M fall round-up was to begin in the morning, and the hands were having a last fling before starting weeks of strenuous work. The atmosphere was lively but without menace.

Buying a drink, he carried the glass across the room with nothing in mind other than passing the evening away. Once he had seen Sheriff Basso in the morning he would hurry back to the DL to, hopefully, put his mind to rest over Letty Dale. By all accounts she had been foolhardy in riding off against Dan Logan's advice, but this didn't prevent Meade from feeling responsible for her.

He paused by an empty chair at a table where four men sat playing cards. Meade could sense a difference here.

There was none of the fun so evident among the cowboys who worked hard and played hard. Set apart from the others in the saloon, the four card-players were not cowpunchers. All of them had eyes as cold and black as the sockets in a skull. The man shuffling the deck of cards raised a hard face to Meade.

'Shall I deal you in, stranger?'

About to decline the offer, Meade held his tongue. These men were not a part of the Running M crew, so what was their business in Tolula? The thought that they were probably part of the rustler gang prompted him give a nod of assent to the question. Maybe he would learn something of help to Dan Logan and Rosie Kirby. He didn't feel it safe to include Buck Woodward.

'I'll try my luck,' he said, taking the vacant chair.

It was a crooked game, Meade discovered after losing forty dollars. Watching carefully, he identified the system they were using. Within a short time he had their measure. After little more than an hour he had regained his forty dollars plus another thirty dollars. There was no conversation, no names were spoken, and the four of them could have been strangers to each other as well as to him. But Meade sensed differently, and he learned he was right when something caused the four men he was playing with to exchange fleeting but meaningful glances.

Covertly watching as he appeared to be concentrating on his hand of cards, Meade assumed that it was the arrival of someone in the saloon that had caused the barely perceptible stir among the four men. Through the crowd he saw the man who had drawn their attention. Standing at the bar, a livid scar across his cheek evident even from a distance, was the slender figure of Cass Gore. Puzzled, Meade watched the small man down a whiskey and turn to leave.

Obviously others beside Rosie Kirby

and himself knew that Gore was a range detective. It came to Meade then that the three rustlers who had come close to hanging him in the night had mistaken him for Cass Gore.

'That's it, stranger,' the man who had invited him to play said, tossing his cards to the centre of the table. The others followed his lead.

They were getting up from their chairs. Meade, who was now fifty dollars up, said, 'I'd sure like to give you fellas a chance to win your money back.'

'Some other time.' The main man showed total indifference as he and the others moved away. Though they tried they couldn't conceal their urgency. Cass Gore was in great danger.

Scooping up his winnings, Meade hurried to the bar. He had to thrust his shoulders into several men to reach a bartender. He got muttered complaints, but no opposition.

'Is there a back way out of here?' Meade asked.

'Through the store there,' the bartender answered, pointing to a door that stood ajar.

Going through, Meade scrambled over barrels and boxes to reach a door leading to the outside. It was locked, so he took a step back and sent it crashing open with a kick. Finding himself in a narrow alleyway, he turned right and ran towards the flickering lights of the main street. Slowing when he reached the end of the alley, he pressed his back tightly against the wall of a building to take a cautious look around.

The Faro Wheel was to his right along the street. To his left, Cass Gore was untying the reins of his horse, which the line of Running M horses had forced him to leave further down the street. Mounting up, Gore headed his horse at a walking pace in the direction of the alley in which Meade was concealed.

'Gore,' Meade called in a whisper, seeing a slight tensing of Gore's body in reaction, 'It's Henry Meade. There's four of them lying for you.'

'I figured there were two,' Gore replied in his detached way, without stopping his horse or showing any sign that Meade was there. 'One's across the street there by the bank.'

Meade looked. The shadows in the doorway of the bank were misshapen. 'I see him.'

'The other's crouching down behind that second trough,' Gore said.

Soon Gore would be out of earshot and on his own. Meade hissed urgently at him, 'The other two must be on this side of the street. Can you see them, Gore?'

'No.'

'Keep looking, Gore. When they make their play, leave the two across the street to me.'

'This doesn't concern you, Meade.'

Gore's whisper was barely audible now, and Meade had to take a chance by raising his voice a little. 'Do as I say, Gore, leave those on your left to me.'

He moved a little towards the street

then, though careful to keep himself in the long shadows cast by the tall building. Watching Gore ride steadily away from him, he had to admire the man. Aware that a trap had been set for him, the range detective would have had a reasonable chance of escape if he had mounted up and galloped in the opposite direction. Probably recognizing that to take such a course would only postpone the inevitable, Gore was putting himself on show to draw out his enemies. He was playing a dangerous game; a very dangerous game.

Nothing happened, and Meade felt the tension in the street increasing. The grating piano music and babble from the saloon was a faint backdrop to the slow, rhythmic clip-clop of the hoofs of Gore's horse. Meade, with his head slanted to avoid being partially blinded by the rise and fall of light from the sizzling lamp outside the Faro Wheel, caught a slight movement.

It was nothing more than the edge of what could be a figure silhouetted by the saloon light behind it. He hesitated, not wanting to shoot what was perhaps some innocent drunk trying to make his way to his horse. Gore was steadily and unwittingly advancing on what Meade had seen. Normally cool and calm in any tough situation, Meade's nerves were wound up tight by the unusual circumstances.

He detected some slight movement in what he was now pretty sure was a partially hidden man. Unable to delay any longer, he fired at the indefinite target. The flash of a gun from the position of Meade's target, almost at the same time as he had pulled the trigger, cancelled out any fear that he had been wrong.

Everything happened at a blurring speed. Gore went down off one side of his horse as if felled by the shot, but he came up on the other side, using the animal as a shield as he fired at someone out of Meade's sight further along the street.

Swinging to his left, Meade fired at

the bank doorway, and was rewarded by the sight and sound of a body hitting the boardwalk hard. A clatter told Meade that a gun about to be fired had been let fall.

A bullet smacked into the wood of the building beside his head. A flash said that it had been fired by the man crouching at the trough. The man switched his fire then, aiming at Gore, who, still exchanging shots with the fourth gunman, had his back to the trough.

Meade recognized that the man's next shot was almost certain to get Gore. With the man too well concealed to be picked off from across the street, Meade raced towards the trough. A bullet plucked at his trouser leg as he drew closer, and he could actually feel the heat of another bullet as it whistled past close to his face. Then he was leaping up in the air, clearing the trough and colliding with the man on the other side. They both went crashing down, each of them disorientated for a moment. The other man was the quicker getting to his feet, but Meade evened things up by lashing out with a kick that caught his opponent in the groin. Groaning in pain, the man doubled over. Leaping to his feet, Meade used his six-shooter as a cosh. He clubbed the man on the back of the head, felling him.

Looking down, he recognized one of the four card players. He was a hard man. With the back of his skull smashed in, he was bringing up a handgun. Slamming his foot down on the wrist of the man's gunhand, Meade kept it there and aimed his own gun at his opponent. Aware that he was about to die, the man looked Meade straight in the eye and bravely smiled a taunting smile. Without compunction, Meade shot him dead centre between the eyes.

Going cautiously back across the street, he joined Gore, who said with satisfaction. 'We got all four, Meade.'

Curious about the gunfire, men were tumbling out of the doors of the saloon, milling around aimlessly, asking each other questions without expecting answers. They spotted Gore and Meade.

'What's all the shooting?' one of them called.

'We're not sure,' Gore answered. 'But a couple of *hombres* just went high-tailing it down towards the livery.'

'Whatever it was, it ain't none of our business,' a cowboy said.

'You're danged right,' another concurred. 'Let's go back in and do some serious drinking.'

Swiftly losing interest, the drinking men went back into the Faro Wheel. But a shout of enquiry came from further up the street. 'What's going on here?'

Jasper Nailham appeared out of the night. The darkness couldn't hide the way age had twisted his body. He hurried up to Gore and Meade. 'Can either of you tell me what in tarnation is happening here?' He peered at Meade in the poor light. 'Say, ain't you the fella wants to see the sheriff?'

'I'll be seeing him in the morning.'

'The morning's the morning,' Jasper said in an annoyed mutter. 'It's tonight what bothers me. What's been happening down here?'

'We heard some shots,' Gore told him.

'I think there could be a couple of bodies across the street, Jasper,' Meade added.

'Gosh darn it, why in tarnation do these things happen when Moses ain't in town!'

As the old man hobbled away from them to investigate, Gore turned to Meade. 'Don't get to thinking this settles anything between us. It was a horse that beat me, not you. There will be another time.'

'I won't need the help of a horse then,' Meade promised.

'Don't fool yourself.'

Having said that, Gore mounted up. Without a word of thanks or a backward glance, he rode off in a direction that would take him out of Tolula.

Staring after him for a moment. Meade moved off before Nailham had a chance to come back across the street. He walked back to the hotel. In the foyer, Ducking, the proprietor, a small man with the severe looks of a bank manager and the nervous twitchings of a jack-rabbit, was behind his desk. The only other person present was Rosie Kirby, who was sitting in an armchair reading a newspaper. As she saw Meade enter, she stood up.

Having only seen her in mannish clothes, Meade was taken aback by her appearance. Long black hair groomed and gleaming, she wore a dress of green silk that made the most of an already perfect figure. Her dark eyes registered the pleasure she got from the way her appearance had affected him.

'Henry Meade,' she greeted him with a tentative smile. 'I heard gunfire and immediately assumed that it would involve you. Did it?'

Delaying his answer, Meade then admitted, 'Yes, Cass Gore was in a fix so I helped him out.'

'Which settles the score between you, I guess,' she commented.

'Not according to Cass Gore,' he said grimly.

'He's a strange man,' she acknowledged, 'but I have faith in his work.'

'The rustlers know about him now, so he'll have a whole heap of problems,' Meade warned.

Rosie Kirby wore a worried frown. 'Perhaps it's time I paid him off. I don't want his death on my conscience, Meade.'

'Cass Gore doesn't strike me as a man who'll give up halfway through a job,' Meade said.

'The situation is getting worse,' she sighed. 'Even you seem a little pensive right now, Meade.'

Meade decided to brighten up the conversation by drawling, 'That's because of you, Miss Kirby. I guess I can't accept that the beautiful lady I see here is the rancher I met out on the range.'

'I am one and the same,' she assured him with a little chuckle. Then her levity disappeared as she added, 'I am the woman who's losing so many head of cattle that the Three Cs will soon be going under. But there's hope, I understand. Dan Logan tells me you're about to become a deputy sheriff.'

'I guess that depends on whether or not Moses Basso goes along with the idea when I see him in the morning,' Meade told her, adding, 'Anyway, I don't really see how a tin star pinned on one man's chest is going to stop this rustling, Miss Kirby.'

'You're right,' she sighed, sitting back down and gesturing for him to take the chair beside her.

'Have you any thoughts on who is behind this rustling, Miss Kirby?'

'Just suspicions,' she answered. 'I suppose most of the rustlers are outsiders, but the way it happens there has to be somebody local organizing it.'

'Buck Woodward?'

Rosie Kirby gave an emphatic shake of her head. 'Definitely not, and that makes it all the worse, Meade. There's two tragedies here, one already happening, the rustling, and the second, which will be much much worse, about to happen at any time. That's where a tin star, if you get to wear it, would come in real useful.'

'You'll have to help me with that, Miss Kirby, I don't get your drift,' Mead queried.

'Old Dan Logan is getting angrier and angrier, Meade. It wouldn't take much to have him ride against Woodward. That'll be a range war, with a lot of killing. I don't want that to happen. No, what I am trying to say is that I want you to stop it from happening.'

Rosie Kirby was frantic with worry, and the next morning Meade found that the same possibility of a range war was uppermost in the mind of Sheriff Moses Basso.

'It would be a bloodbath, Meade,' he

said despondently after going through a short ritual and pinning a star on Meade's chest. 'Old Dan's been hankering after a set-to with Buck Woodward for a mighty long time. I've had a double job of work upholding the law and keeping the peace between them two. Buck ain't looking for trouble, but you can only push a man so far, and Dan Logan's been shoving Woodward for too long. The doc says I can't get back in the saddle for some time yet, so I'm glad to have you around.'

'I reckon as how Dan Logan won't listen to me the way he would you, Sheriff,' Meade said.

'That old mule won't listen to anyone, Meade,' Basso disagreed. 'The real answer is to stop the cattle-thieving, then Dan won't have nothing to get ornery about. He told me that you been keeping an eye on things for him at the DL round-up. You pick up any sign as to who might be running the rustling?'

‘I saw enough to have me believe that the old man could be right,’ Meade said to test Basso’s reaction.

‘Buck Woodward?’

Meade was surprised. Rosie Kirby had been sure that Woodward couldn’t be involved, yet the sheriff didn’t seem about to argue. He replied, ‘Yes, Buck Woodward.’

‘You may be right, though it goes against the grain to say so, as Buck’s been a friend of mine for years. It sure looks like it’s somebody from round here,’ Basso mused. ‘It’s for you to find out now, Meade. You’re the man wearing the badge.’

‘It’s not going to be easy, Sheriff,’ Meade said, making for the door when Basso surprised him with an unconnected question.

‘This girl you rode in with, Meade, who claims to be Dan Logan’s grandchild. I’m sure I know her from someplace. What can you tell me about her?’

This worried Meade. The plan was

going well, but it seemed possible that Basso could ruin everything. He replied cautiously. 'Letty and me don't go back no further than Raimondo. That's where I met her.'

'Yet you're saying she's Logan's kin?' a dubious sheriff questioned.

'She convinced me, Sheriff,' Meade said, noticing as he went out of the office that Moses Basso looked anything but convinced.

7

'I'd like you to fill your glasses, folks,' Dan Logan said, standing at the end of the long table from which the Chinese cook and his wife self-effacingly cleared the remnants of a veritable feast. 'As most of you will know, it is customary on this occasion to drink to business in the coming year. Tonight, if you good folk will bear with me, I'd like you also to join a happy man by raising your glasses to welcome my beautiful granddaughter, Letty.'

With Letty sitting at his left side, Meade was conscious of her embarrassment as all eyes turned her way. On his right, Rosie Kirby spoke quietly from the corner of her mouth. 'At least old Dan's not mentioned either the cattle stealing or Buck Woodward.'

'One and the same thing,' Meade grinned as he repeated one of Logan's favourite phrases, getting a low and lilting laugh from Rosie.

But it was no time for joking. The round-ups of the DL and the Three Cs showed that even all of the unbranded mavericks had been rustled. Dan Logan and Rosie Kirby were faced with the bleak prospect of dwindling herds and declining profits. Somewhere out on the range, perhaps Cass Gore, and maybe Buck Woodward knew just where, though with different interests, the running irons were constantly hot and the branding fires blazed day and night. Meade admired old man Logan for keeping clear of the subject on this night of supposed celebration.

Meade had learned that this dinner was an annual tradition on the completion of the DL and Three Cs round-ups. It was held at the Logan and Kirby ranch houses on alternate years. The absence of the district's third big rancher, Buck Woodward, was noticeable. He thought, too, of Cass Gore, who had calmly resumed his duties and was right now in the bunkhouse with the rest of the DL hands. Now that the rustlers, whoever they were, knew him to be a range detective, Gore's life wasn't worth a plugged nickel.

The huge room they were in had been specially decorated. There was an elegance to the proceedings throughout, a decorum unexpected in the home of a rough diamond cattleman. Dan Logan had gone to a lot of trouble and expense to make this evening a special event. Meade didn't doubt that the old man had been largely motivated by his delight at having Letty there.

The other guests were Ikey Kindler, the store-keeper and his wife, a small woman with a twittering manner that Meade found to be irritating, Charles Casson, whose dislike of Meade had been exacerbated by him having been made a deputy sheriff, and Moses Basso, whose eyes studied Letty inquisitively as she was toasted.

Meade thought how girlishly pretty

Letty looked in a yellow and black checkered Dolly Varden dress. Illumination from the kerosene lamps around the room deepened the rich golden tan of her face and put an extra twinkle in her large brown eyes. In her unselfish way, she leaned towards him to say, 'I feel terrible about my grand — about Myrtle being upstairs away from all this.'

Not the sort to be able to sustain a lie for long, Letty had got caught up in the illusion of her relationship to the Logans. Aware that she had come to love her bogus grandfather and grandmother, Meade was relieved by the thought that Letty would continue their charade because of this. Yet in another way he felt guilty, and he was more and more frequently going through periods of regret at having started the deception.

'Myrtle is too ill to enjoy something like this,' Rosie Kirby, overhearing what Letty had said, put in, 'but I confess I don't like thinking about her being up there all alone.'

'I think I'll pop up and see how she is,' Letty said, feeling it was permissible to leave the table because the Kindler woman was going across to sit at a piano, her movements those of a pecking bird as she ran her fingers over the keys. To Meade's pleased astonishment she proved herself to be a brilliant musician as she began to play 'Beautiful Dreamer'.

Soothed by the music, Meade watched a frowning Basso observe Letty keenly as she left the room. When Rosie Kirby spoke, Meade had to recycle her words in his head before being able to grasp what she had said.

'I know that I'm prying, Meade, but I have good reason for doing so,' Rosie was saying. 'Are you involved, for want of a better word, with Dan's granddaughter?'

That evening, Rosie Kirby looked more like the untamed woman Meade had first met out on the range. Coming to the DL on horseback meant her having to exchange the glamorous dress she had worn in Tolula for a black-buttoned red merino shirt and a divided skirt.

'No,' he shook his head. 'I just found her and brought her here.'

'There is a reward, I understand.'

Meade studied her sharply for a moment, expecting her to be judging him, but she wasn't. 'Yes. I'm going to use it to start up my own ranch.'

'Around here?'

'No, back where I came from.'

Knowing his type too well to enquire where that was, Rosie Kirby said, 'I could make life simpler for you, Meade. Jack Milton, my foreman, is an old man who wants out. He's too loyal to leave me in the lurch. What I'm offering you is a position as ramrod of the Three Cs.'

'It's right kind of you to ask me, Miss Kirby,' Meade chose his words carefully so as not to hurt her, 'but I'm hankering after my own place, not being straw boss for someone else.'

Turning her face away at an angle

from him, she said softly, 'Maybe you wouldn't be just a foreman for very long.'

'Is that a proposition, Miss Kirby?'

'That makes me sound like some kind of dance-hall girl,' she said, her face reddening. 'Perhaps the word *proposal* is more fitting.'

Though this sort of thing would be shocking back East, it was a necessary part of the bluntness of life out here. Rosie Kirby was a competent business-woman, but she knew that the Three Cs needed a man in charge. Out West, with necessity digging in the spurs, there was no time for niceties, for courtship. A barren social life meant that suitors were few and far between. Opportunities were so rare they had to be evaluated in a business rather than a romantic sense.

Too staggered to find words to continue the conversation, Meade was rescued by the return of Letty, who whispered in Meade's ear as Dan Logan arrived to begin a conversation with Rosie Kirby.

'Sheriff Basso is watching me all the time, Henry.'

'He told me that he thought he knew you from somewhere, Letty.'

'What if he remembers?'

'What can he remember?' Meade asked logically.

'If he did see you somewhere, then that doesn't stop you from being Dan Logan's granddaughter.'

'No . . . ' Letty murmured, too fearful to accept what Meade had said.

'Don't worry, Letty. A Cheyenne medicine-man couldn't alter Dan Logan's mind about you now.'

'I hope you're right, Henry,' Letty said wistfully, saying no more because Logan had called to Meade.

The old man's face wore a mixed expression of anger and excitement. He was flanked by Moses Basso and Charles Casson, both of their faces serious. Ikey Kindler's wife was playing 'Home Sweet Home' on the piano, while the Chinese couple placed a huge jug of steaming coffee and cups on the table.

The company ignored the hot drink as Dan Logan addressed Meade. 'Charles tells me a couple of the boys just rode in to report having seen a fire burning in the distance at Misty Sink Creek, up on the west range, Henry.'

'Either saddle tramps or rustlers,' Charles Casson said. 'My money's on it being rustlers. The Running M round-up is still under way.'

With an anxious glance to see how Dan Logan had reacted to this inflammatory suggestion, Sheriff Basso cautioned the ranch foreman. 'It won't help none for any of us to go jumping the gun, Charles.'

'There you go again, Moses,' Logan complained. 'You'd still argue for Buck Woodward if you found him with a red-hot running iron in his hand.'

'That ain't likely to happen, Dan,' Basso said.

'Maybe it will, maybe it won't,' Logan argued. 'The thing is, this here's a good chance to catch some cattle-thief redhanded. Take Charles and three or four of the men up there with you, Henry.'

'Best if I go alone, Dan,' Meade said evenly. 'I'm the one wearing the badge, so I guess this is my play.'

'I'd like to go along,' Casson volunteered.

Moses Basso agreed with an energetic nod. 'Take Charles with you, Meade. If I was fit I wouldn't go out there alone.'

'He won't be alone,' Rosie Kirby spoke up. 'I was about to head for home, and it won't be far out of my way to take in Misty Sink Creek.'

'But . . . ' Meade started to protest, but Rosie stopped him firmly.

'But you don't want a woman along, is that what you were about to say, Meade? Dan Logan or Moses Basso can vouch for me. I can blast a tick off a steer's backside at forty yards.'

'It still don't make sense,' Casson protested. 'Misty Sink is one long way from the Three Cs ranch house. Why don't you just ride along with us to Crevasse Fork, Miss Kirby, then go on your way home?'

'I'll do no such thing,' a determined Rosie told the foreman.

'You're calling the shots, Henry,' Dan Logan said impatiently. 'Why not take Rosie and Charles along?'

'I don't want there to be more than two of us, so I guess Miss Kirby better ride with me,' Meade made his decision. Casson would be of more use if things got rough out on the range, but it was a long ride to the creek, and he much preferred Rosie's company to that of the sour foreman.

Coming up close to him, Letty surreptitiously reached for Meade's hand, her fingers entwining with his as she whispered, 'Please take care, Henry.'

'I'll be fine, Letty,' he said, giving her hand a reassuring squeeze before releasing it.

Leaving a disgruntled Casson behind

them, they went out with Dan Logan calling out a few last words. 'This is the big chance to put an end to the cow stealing. I'm relying on you, Henry.'

Making no reply, Meade saddled up while Rosie took a mantle from a saddle-bag on her polka-dot horse. Putting the garment across her shoulders as a protection against the cold of night, she swung lithely up into the saddle.

As they rode, Meade having to control the exuberance of his great chestnut horse, the tense silence of the night broken only by a short burst of frantic neighing from the corral, he asked, 'How do you see it, Miss Kirby?'

'It would suit me better if you called me Rosie . . . Henry. You mean when we reach the creek?'

'Yes.'

'My guess is that it could be a small band of the rustlers working that end of the range. It won't be anything to do with Buck.'

As they rode upward, the trail turned

slightly and they moved out through scattered pinewood into open range. Rosie softly hummed 'Beautiful Dreamer', the tune they had earlier heard played on the piano.

Recalling the offer she had made him, Meade commented, 'I figured you and Woodward to be real close, Rosie.'

'Not in the way I think you mean,' she replied pensively. 'Buck's a good neighbour and a good friend, but that's all he can ever be as far as I'm concerned.'

'Is that the way he sees it?'

'Never asked him, so I couldn't tell you, Henry. But that makes no difference. It takes two to make that sort of a deal.'

That was true. Though she evidently was ready to make a commitment to him, Meade wasn't sure that he was. Rosie Kirby was a beautiful woman, and she came with a ready-made ranch, but he wasn't sure that was enough. Maybe it would work on a short-term basis. An agreement to spend all of the rest of their lives together was something else.

'I guess I was pretty stupid asking you to join the Three Cs,' Rosie said ruefully. 'With Letty around I should have known better.'

'As I told you, Rosie, all that's between Letty and me is that I brought her here to Tolula,' he spoke firmly, though he was sure that she didn't believe him. He was far from certain that he could believe himself.

The two of them rode on in silence then, taking the left trail on reaching Crevasse Fork. An hour later, Meade was alerted as he saw the ears of Rosie's polka-dot lie back. The horse had sensed danger somewhere in the darkness. Then the bawling of a solitary cow broke the stillness, a signal that they were closing in on their destination at the edge of the range. They reined into a little jackpine hollow and dismounted. Rosie took a .30–30 Winchester from her saddle holster.

They moved off on foot through a

sage-panoplied region of knolls and low ridges interspersed with small grassy areas and springy patches. As they slowly paced they disturbed a grey-brown sage-hen that flew up with a loud beating of wings. Meade paid a silent tribute to Rosie Kirby's strong nerves when she remained completely calm.

A brilliant moon came to their aid, slowly pushing its way above the bulk of a range of rolling hills. Moonlight traced a silver ribbon on a stream. Now that they were here he feared for Rosie's safety. Personal experience of the rustlers told him that she mustn't fall into their hands.

They silently dropped down to lie belly-flat on the ground, looking down at the little creek. Meade could see only two cows. Maybe another animal stood in the shadows, but he wasn't sure. That explained why the fire the DL hands had seen was no longer burning. It wouldn't take long to rebrand a couple of cows. It annoyed Meade that he had come all this way just to find himself on the petty fringe of the cattle-stealing. All he could salvage from the operation was to capture and question the men responsible.

As they kept watch, a man emerged from the shadows cast by dead poplars standing in line like wooden skeletons. Moving stealthily, he came down to the creek. Crouching, he half-immersed a water bottle and held it while it slowly filled. Meade estimated that the man was about to move out, and the fact he was replenishing a single bottle said that he was alone.

The man stood up. He was huge, and in the light of the moon he looked like a hold-over from the Stone Age. His sloping shoulders were inhuman in their spread, and there was no semblance of a neck to support the shaven head that was set on his massive frame. The sight of him was one of bestial power.

He cautiously looked around. Knowing that the man could only hope to see movement in the half-light, spot a change in the various horizons, Meade remained perfectly still. But when the rustler turned his probing gaze their way, Rosie instinctively ducked her head. Meade saw the big body jerk in alarm, then the man was running back towards the poplars, where he must have left his horse.

'What's happening?' Rosie asked as Meade jumped to his feet.

'He's about to ride out. I'm going to get my horse to head him off,' Meade answered. 'You stay here and keep down.'

Meade was up in the saddle and bringing the chestnut round when he saw the big man come riding out into the open. He headed for him, not slackening speed as he neared a placid pool of brown water. The water-hole was overhung on all sides by tangled scrub. To go round would mean losing his man. Sending the chestnut straight at the pool, Meade pulled the magnificent beast up at just the right moment.

The horse soared high over the water and landed to gallop ahead without breaking pace.

He saw the big man jerk the head of his black horse to the right as he raced away from the creek. The rustler had a start on Meade that would quickly widen if the distance between them wasn't closed at once.

Swinging round the jutting cliff that walled the northern entrance to the creek, Meade was aware of the chestnut's head coming up and its ears flattening in readiness. Digging in his heels and at the same time flinging his body forward to the right of the saddlehorn, Meade launched his 1200 pound thoroughbred at the black horse and its rider. Meade was using the terrific *golpe de caballo* that was practised by the *vaqueros* of the south.

There was no protection from the impact as the big chestnut struck the black horse with its full weight. The black went down as if it had been shot. Floundering and squealing in pain and fright, it skidded on its side back towards the creek, its rider clinging on until he was thrown clear. Leaping from the saddle, Meade landed on the big man's chest.

He was reaching for where he imagined the throat should be in the short neck, when a fist the size of a ham came swinging up. The blow caught Meade on the jaw, sending him flying backwards off the big man. They both reached their feet at the same time, both armed but neither having the chance to draw a gun.

Realizing that he had to win the fight early or not at all, Meade waded in to connect a left and a right with his antagonist's chin. Neither punch rocked the big man in the slightest. A thick pair of arms was wrapped around Meade, squeezing him so hard that he could feel his ribs compressed close to what had to be breaking point. Unable to breathe, it came as a relief to be lifted clear off the ground and slammed down upon his back.

His opponent moved in on him, but Meade neatly tripped him. Springing up while the big man still lay face down, Meade stamped hard on the back of the round, shaven head. Feeling the impact up through his leg, Meade could detect the moment when the face gave way as it was mashed into the ground. With a roar of rage the giant came up onto his feet, his face bloodied and pulped.

Stepping forwards, Meade beat a fast tattoo of punches into the hard body, then switched to the head. Without retaliation, he ripped home punch after punch. All he succeeded in doing was damaging the bleeding face more and smearing his own hurting knuckles with blood. Taking one step back, Meade arranged his feet for maximum leverage as he sent a straight right punch that contained all of his power into the centre of the big man's face. Blood and pus flew in all directions, and lumps of flesh with pieces of jagged white bone protruding from them, were dislodged from the mangled face. But the big man was not shaken at all. He used one elbow to catch Meade just below the ear and put him down on one knee.

Breathing hard, his strength diminished by the hard punches he had thrown without effect, Meade knew that he would never put the giant down by use of his fists. Glancing quickly round he saw a large stone to his left. Judging that he could lift it with both hands, he promised himself that he would use it as a weapon at the first opportunity.

Head tucked even further down into his wide shoulders, the man was coming at him. Sensing that his antagonist intended to aim a kick at his head, Meade dropped flat from the kneeling position to use both legs to once again neatly trip the giant. Seeing him go crashing down, Meade jumped up and grabbed the stone.

It was so heavy that he had difficulty raising it above his head with both hands. This gave his opponent time to get to his knees. Moving close, swaying a little from the over-balancing weight of the stone, he used both arms to throw it straight down at the shaven head.

Raising one muscle-packed arm, the giant deflected the stone as easily as he would have brushed aside a rubber ball. The stone that would have shattered the armbone of any other man, hit the ground harmlessly, yards away.

Determined to fight on for as long as he could, though aware that he was already defeated, Meade managed to land a left jab to the face before two stunning punches to the side of his head sent him reeling.

Pausing to use one hand to tentatively probe the considerable damage to his face, satisfied that he could end this fight whenever he wished, the huge man got the measure of the weak and shaken Meade with a straight left punch, then launched his right hand.

With no energy left to take avoiding action, Meade watched the massive fist coming towards him. Though he knew that it must be coming at a great speed, it seemed to be taking ages. Resigned to his fate, he was surprised to see the fist stop in mid air as the giant became as immobile as a statue. Then the big man was toppling backwards while at the same time Meade heard the crack of a rifle shot.

The rustler landed on his back with a crash. Looking up, Meade saw Rosie Kirby standing on a ledge with a still smoking Winchester rifle held under one arm.

'You got him,' Meade appreciatively called to her.

'Right between the eyes,' she said.

'I don't think so,' Meade said doubtfully, going over to look for a bullet hole somewhere on the gigantic dead body.

He was still looking when Rosie came up beside him. With an expression of distaste on her lovely face, she used the toe of her right boot to part the skin and flesh ripped to pieces when Meade had pushed the man's face into the ground. Her toe cleared the flesh away so that the white bone of the forehead was revealed. An amazed Meade saw a hole made by a rifle bullet dead centre through the bone.

'Like I said, right between the eyes,' Rosie Kirby said. She identified the dead man. 'He's Sol Bartlett, one of Buck Woodward's men.'

'I could have done with him alive,' Meade murmured.

Rosie told him what he recognized as the truth. 'If I'd let him live, Henry, you would be dead now.'

8

'I won't deny that Bartlett worked for me, Meade, but what you caught him at was off his own hook. He weren't the first to go in for a bit of moonlighting, and I don't suppose he'll be the last. I sure would have fired him if you hadn't killed him.'

Buck Woodward brought over two glasses of whiskey and placed one on the table in front of Meade before sitting down. Unlike the grandiose two-storey Logan home, the Running M ranch house was a veranda-surrounded bungalow. But it was spacious, impressive and well kept, despite the obvious signs that it was occupied by a bachelor. An affable Woodward seemed very different to how Meade remembered from the night he had rescued him from the lynching party out on the range. Though he was every bit as tough and capable now as he had been then, his role of host seemed to have smoothed the man's rougher edges. Meade assumed it was the change of environment that was responsible for the difference.

Taking a sip of whiskey from his glass, Meade struggled to sound casual as he enquired, 'Have you finished your round-up, Woodward?'

'Now why didn't you just ask outright if I lost any beef?' an amused Woodward grinned.

'Did you?'

'Not one head, aside from the usual expected wastage,' Buck Woodward replied, 'which ain't bad considering we're speaking of ten thousand cows. Now I know that seems suspicious in itself, seeing as how Logan and Rosie Kirby suffered big losses, but if I had anything to hide, pard, then it would be easier for me to lie and say I was losing out to rustlers same as the other two.'

That sounded logical, but Woodward was a clever man who might be putting himself above suspicion by admitting that he was not a victim of the cattle-thieving, while claiming that he knew of no reason why this should be.

'I'm looking at it from all angles,' Meade said.

Inclining his head to show his acceptance of Meade's attitude, Woodward said, 'I reckon you are, pard, and there's something about you tells me you were once a cattleman yourself. You know that a rancher is as much a gambler as the white-faced, well-dressed dealer in a saloon poker game. It's after all the yahoo and fuss of the annual round-up that he counts his chips to find out whether he's won or lost. I've come out a winner again this year, pard, but these rustlers stop me from feeling good. Dan Logan and Rosie Kirby have worked just as hard as me, and they don't deserve to lose a single steer.'

'Dan Logan wouldn't believe his ears if he heard you say that, Woodward.'

'Dan Logan wouldn't believe *me* if

he heard me say that,' Woodward corrected Meade. 'What I'm saying is that it would be for the best if you took no notice of Logan. Do things Moses Basso's way.'

'I do things my way,' Meade said in a low, firm tone.

'You have to do your own thing, but it might not be healthy to get carried away by that new tin star you're wearing, pard.'

'Sounds like you're threatening me, Woodward.'

'If that's how it seems to you, then you heard me wrong,' Woodward hastily explained, refilling both glasses to show there was no animosity. 'What I'm saying is that you could waste a whole heap of time looking in the wrong direction.'

What was Woodward implying? Rosie Kirby came into Meade's mind. She'd hired Cass Gore, but maybe Gore wasn't what he was said to be. Liking the woman, Meade couldn't imagine Rosie as queen of the rustlers, but he had known more unlikely things. Against her was the way she had shot Sol Bartlett. She was right in saying the big man would probably have killed Meade if she hadn't stopped him, but if Rosie was good enough with a rifle to drill Bartlett between the eyes, then she could have put him out of action by winging him. It could be that she had wanted to silence the rustler lest he implicate her. But it didn't add up. Maybe she was faking her own losses as a cover-up, but that would make Dan Logan the sole victim of the rustlers. The Running M offered rich pickings for the cattle-thieves.

'Are you saying you know in which direction I should be looking, Woodward?' Meade asked.

Taking a drink before answering, Woodward replaced his glass noisily on the table. 'Where you do your hunting is up to you. All I'm saying is that I got my own ideas, but I'm not confident enough to share what I know with you right now.'

'You'll call me when you are sure?'

Woodward shook his head. 'I won't need to do that, pard. You can come a-running when you hear the gunfire and smell the gunsmoke.'

'Maybe I'll get there first,' Meade said.

'If you do, then I'll be the first to shake you by the hand,' Woodward said, getting to his feet as Meade stood up from the table, ready to leave. 'You heading for the DL shindig in Tolula?'

'Yes,' Meade nodded. Round-ups were hard work. Dan Logan, having held his own celebration at the ranch house, was showing appreciation of his hands by putting a sum of money behind the bar of the Faro Wheel for the DL cowboys to have a good night. The fact that the men were beginning to accept him, and even his relationship with Charles Casson seemed to be improving, made Meade feel that he had to put in an appearance. Extra to this he would welcome a word with Cass Gore. He'd like to learn if the range detective's investigation had made progress.

'You're a man I'd like to take a drink with, pard,' Woodman surprised Meade by saying, 'but I allow I wouldn't be real welcome in town tonight. Some other time perhaps.'

He surprised Meade for a second time, by offering his hand. Meade took it. The handshake was the firm one of a genuine man. It put the finishing touch to the good impression Meade had gained of Woodward, and he mentioned this to Moses Basso an hour later when he sat in the sheriff's office.

'I always reckoned Buck, Henry, but an open mind goes with the badge you wear,' Basso pointed out. 'We've never had rustling on this scale. Rosie and Dan will be finished if it goes on. It's got to be stopped, whether it's Buck, which I doubt, or someone else we know, has got to be hurt in the process.'

Meade agreed with this. It was dark outside now and sounds of merrymaking at the saloon filtered into the office.

He said to Basso, 'I'm going to look in on the boys at the Faro Wheel, Moses, you fancy coming along?'

'No, you go ahead,' the sheriff answered. 'I get tuckered out real easy since getting shot up. Old Dan wants me out at the DL for that meeting of his later tonight. You going to be there, Henry?'

'I'll be there,' Meade replied. Dan Logan had called a get-together with Rosie Kirby, Basso, Casson and himself to plan an effective policy for beating the rustlers. 'I won't stay long in the saloon, so I'll call back here for you and we can ride out together.'

'That will suit me fine, Henry,' Basso said. 'That shooting took more out of me than I care to admit. Maybe I won't ever get back to being sheriff again, and it makes me feel better to know that there'll be a good man to replace me.'

'Don't count on that, Moses,' Meade warned. 'I've got other plans.'

The disappointment on the sheriff's face stabbed Meade with guilt as he went out into the night.

When he entered the Faro Wheel he was confronted by a joyful but crazy scene. It didn't pay Ned Farrar, the proprietor, to keep more than two dance-hall girls, and they were two too many during many months of the year. Now, with the boots of drunken, prancing cowboys crushing their toes, and pained expressions on their faces, the two girls were being grabbed and pulled at by whooping, laughing, DL hands. Other cowboys were dancing wildly with each other, but it was Charles Casson who astonished Meade.

The normally aloof foreman was totally uninhibited. A table had been placed close to the saloon pianist. Standing on this was a young fellow playing a violin, while beside him, beating time by slapping his hands against his thighs, a smiling Casson enthusiastically but untunefully sang 'Oh! Susanna'. Those cowboys not dancing were grinning and shouting friendly encouragement to the ramrod they despised when back at the ranch.

Seeing Cass Gore leaning on the bar, Meade walked over to him. Gore, without making any indication that he had seen Meade arrive, called to the bartender for another glass, and pushed a bottle of whiskey so that it came to rest on the counter in front of Meade.

'I guess I owe you a drink, Meade,' Gore said.

This was Gore's first acknowledgment of Meade's assistance in the night-time shoot-out in the street outside. Meade poured himself a drink, watching Gore glance cautiously behind him. He asked, 'What are you looking for?'

'Just checking you haven't brought a horse along to back you up,' Gore replied comically but without smiling. He drank from a glass held in a small, almost effeminate hand. Meade thought it amazing that so delicate a hand could deliver so devastating a punch. There was no doubting though that the well-shaped hands and sensitive fingers had an affinity with the ivory-handled guns at Gore's lean waist.

'Aren't you ever going to forget that, Gore?'

'I couldn't do that, Meade,' Gore said, going on to say, 'No man has ever beaten me at anything.'

Meade realized that Gore was stating a fact and not boasting. He said, 'I guess I spoilt your record.'

'Nope,' Gore shook his head. 'All you did, Meade, was raise a question. It's a question that you and me have got to find the answer to one day.'

'Does it mean that much to you, Gore?'

'It does.'

'I'm happy for it to be a question that remains unanswered,' Meade said.

'I'm not.'

Irritated by the subject, Meade looked over to where Casson was now singing 'Jim Crack Corn' as animatedly as he had the first song. He commented to Gore, 'Casson's got to be at a meeting with Dan Logan later. I sure hope he isn't too liquored-up to make it.'

'Casson isn't drunk,' Gore informed him.

'He sure looks that way to me.'

'No, I've seen men like it before. Whenever they get among people like this they have to be up front, showing off. They're odd. I prefer drunks.'

'You make a real study of people, Gore,' Meade complimented his temporary companion.

'I've found it vital in my line of work,' Gore said, adding sombrely, 'The problem is it makes it easier to know who to kill, but harder to do the killing.'

'You've got a strange outlook on life,' Meade remarked.

'Maybe, but I'm still alive,' Gore shrugged. 'What about you, Meade, how much longer have you got amongst the living?'

Caught off balance by the question, Meade came back with a question of his own. 'Are you still on about that kick from a horse, Gore?'

'No, it's nothing to do with that,' Gore said, turning his face to find Meade's eyes and holding them with his. 'You're getting in the way of things, Meade. The cattle-thieves had it all their own way, and Dan Logan and the Kirby woman had no chance until you showed up.'

'What are you saying, Gore?'

'Just that you need to watch your back,' Gore replied.

Wanting to question the man further, Meade was prevented from doing so by Charles Casson. Face red and beaded with sweat from his energetic singing, the foreman had a close to humble air about him as he came up and spoke to Meade.

'We ain't sort of got on since you've been about here, Meade, and I'll confess most of the fault is mine,' Casson said. 'That being so, I'd be obliged if you'd have a drink with me.'

The foreman turned to extend his offer to Gore, but the slim man had moved away. Meade accepted. 'I'll drink with you, Casson. Good thing to clear the air before we get to talking with the others out at the ranch.'

'I agree. We can do more for the DL together than we can apart.' Casson had a contented look as he ordered the drinks. 'We've got to thrash something out tonight, Meade, otherwise the DL and the Three Cs will lose out to the rustlers. I don't intend to let that happen. It's not just because I'd be out of a job, but Dan Logan's been real good to me over the years since he took me on as straw boss. If it comes to riding against the Running M, will you be with us, Meade?'

'If it comes to that,' Meade said, downing the drink Casson had bought him, asking, 'Will you have a drink with me before I ride out?'

'Give me an hour and I'll ride out with you,' Casson offered, a man completely changed by this social occasion. 'I've got something planned for the boys, and I'd like to be here to see them enjoy it.'

'You stay and have your fun, Casson. I'm meeting Moses Basso right away, and we'll be heading out together. Can I get you a drink before I leave?'

Casson's face registered his disappointment. 'I'll take that drink with you, then see you out at the ranch house.'

With the second drink seemingly strengthening the unexpected bond between Casson and himself, Meade looked around the saloon for Gore before he left. There was no sign of the lightly built range detective. Pondering on this, Meade went out, mounted up and moved his horse at walking pace towards the sheriff's office. He could see the note pinned to the door on his approach, and swung down from the saddle to read:

Henry
I'm riding out to the DL early because I don't find it easy in the saddle these days, and would slow you down too much. Maybe you'll

catch up with me. If not, I'll see you there, friend.

Moses Basso

Appreciating how much trouble the sheriff's serious wound was still causing him, Meade could understand his reasons for going on ahead. Getting back up into the saddle, he rode out of Tolula. It wasn't so light a night as when Rosie Kirby and he had ridden up on Sol Bartlett. Now a weak moon flitted like a white moth between broken clouds as he rode along the sloping, open oval in the bottom of the wide canyon that the main-travelled road out of town passed through an hour's ride out of town.

To westward was a dark slope that was dotted with junipers and ribbed by rocky reefs that thrust upward, pointing to where a tall, grey-black cliff rose precipitously.

Some sixth sense made Meade suddenly tense. His chestnut was uneasy, too. Maybe the horse had picked up a sense of alarm from him, or perhaps Meade had caught a contagious feeling of danger from the horse. Whichever it was made no difference. Meade knew that caution was needed, and he remembered the warning Cass Gore had given. He reined in for a moment to listen. There was no sound that didn't fit in with the night. Still half-convinced that danger lurked up on the craggy ridges, Meade found the shadows under the trees were teasing his imagination.

Moving the chestnut on, he could actually feel its reluctance. The horse stumbled momentarily and he leaned over to whisper reassuringly to the animal. Meade passed out of a clump of trees. There was enough moon to cast a yellow glint on the saddle-horn, which meant that when he was crossing the stream up ahead he would be fully exposed to anyone watching from up on the hill.

The tension was mounting so that he could distinctly feel that his horse was trembling. But onwards was the only way to go. Shoes clinking against a rocky surface, the chestnut started across the stream. Nothing happened, and, halfway across, Meade was ready to believe that he had been scaring himself unnecessarily.

He was across the narrow stream when it happened. The heavy darkness high up on the ridges was gashed by the red flare of a rifle being fired. With his reflexes and survival instinct working perfectly and in unison, Meade was throwing himself out of the saddle even before the sound of the shot reached him. But a bullet slammed into his left thigh, stopping his fast, sideways dismount, and throwing him backwards out of the saddle.

Crashing jarringly on to the hard bed of the stream, he lay half-stunned, watching the shallow water turn dark from the blood leaking from his injured leg.

The sound of approaching hoofbeats forced him to rapidly gather his senses.

A few yards from him, the faithful chestnut stood waiting, harness jingling as it violently shook its head either from cold or shock. With the hoofbeats nearer, Meade put a probing hand to his holster. His gun was still there. Turning on to his side, he propped himself up on one elbow and drew the six-shooter. There were two horses, and Meade couldn't understand why they were coming along the route he had taken out of town. With a thumb he eased back the hammer of his gun, ready for any eventuality.

The hoofbeats stopped and a voice called guardedly out of the darkness, 'Are you there, Meade?'

'I'm here,' Meade, recognizing Charles Casson's voice, answered.

'You hurt bad, Meade?'

'Just a flesh wound in the leg, but I'm losing blood.'

Casson came riding up then. With him was a scrawny young cowpuncher Meade had seen among the DL crew, but had never spoken to. Both men dismounted and came over to lift Meade out of the stream and lay him on the grass.

Pulling out a knife to slice open the leg of Meade's trousers, Casson peered at the wound. 'You're lucky it's a poor moon tonight, Meade, or this slug would be right through your heart.' He turned to the cowboy. 'Give me your neckerchief, Lester.'

With his own neckerchief and that of the cowhand, Casson stopped the bleeding by bandaging Meade's wound and applying a tourniquet. He and Lester lifted Meade to his feet.

'Where did the shot come from, Meade, up on the ridge?'

'Yes.'

'That figures,' Casson nodded, squinting up at the ridge in the darkness. 'That's Running M territory. Can you put your weight on that leg?'

Trying tentatively, Meade found it was less painful than he had anticipated. 'I can use the leg fine, Casson.'

'Good. Me and Lester'll get you up

on your horse. You ride on to the DL, and we'll take a scout round up there to see if we can find anything.'

Alone again, and though not expecting more trouble, Meade kept his rifle across the saddle in front of him as he rode.

* * *

Watching the shining brass pendulum of Dan Logan's tall clock swing to and fro, Letty Dale fervently wished that Meade would arrive at the ranch house. Logan and Rosie Kirby were standing together at a table on which a chart had been laid out. They were engaged in a friendly argument over boundaries between their land. This left Moses Basso at a loose end. The sheriff had hardly taken his eyes off Letty since he'd arrived at the DL. Now he walked over and sat next to her.

'I always pride myself on never forgetting a face, Miss Dale,' he said in a manner which told her that this was the first shot in a verbal volley.

'Do you?' She said lamely, as there was nothing else she could say.

'I had occasion a long time ago,' Basso went on, his eyes seeming to look inwards to view the past, 'to check up on an Indian agent. This fellow had a squaw for a wife and an adopted little white daughter. Now I'd swear before Almighty God, Miss Dale, that that little girl was you.'

Trembling inside, Letty managed to keep cool and calm on the outside. She imagined Henry Meade telling her she could bluff her way through this. 'It could well be, Sheriff Basso. I was raised by a couple such as you describe. I've never known who my parents were.'

'Now there's another coincidence.' Basso sounded incredulous. 'A few years before that I was riding with a US marshal's posse who shot and killed a bank raider by the name of Kendow. A woman worked with him. The only name I had for her was Kate. She got away from us, but left a baby girl behind. The marshal took that baby to the reservation and the agent agreed to look after it.'

'What are you saying, Sheriff?' Letty gasped.

'I'm saying, Miss Dale, that you can't be no kin of Dan Logan,' Basso said quietly. 'You seem like a nice young lady, and I've come to like and respect Henry Meade, but that won't allow me to let you fool Dan Logan. I'm giving you warning that — '

Basso broke off as the door opened and a wounded Meade limped in. As Letty joined Rosie in fussing over him, Meade explained that he had been bushwhacked on his way from Tolula. Dan Logan and Moses Basso muttered in impotent anger.

'Rest assured, Henry,' Logan said, 'that whoever did this won't get away with it.'

'I'll ride into town and fetch the doc out here,' Rosie Kirby announced, reaching for her coat.

'I don't need a doctor, it's only a

flesh wound,' Meade protested. 'My leg will be a bit stiff in the morning, but nothing else.'

'Who wrapped it up for you?' Dan Logan enquired.

'Casson came along with a kid named Lester.'

'Where's Casson now, Henry?' Basso asked. 'He's supposed to be here for the meeting.'

'He and the kid went off to see if they could find who drygulched me,' Meade explained.

'That's Charles,' Logan grinned. 'He's like a coyote gnawing at a carcass, just won't give up.'

'I'd like it better if he had given up on this tonight, Dan,' Basso said unhappily. 'Casson's a good man, but he won't be a match for whoever's carrying out this rustling.'

'I'll ride out again to look for him,' Meade decided.

'And I'll go with you,' Basso volunteered.

'No!' Dan Logan commanded in a

half shout. 'You might be fit enough to go riding tomorrow, Henry, but not tonight. As for you, Moses, it will be a long time before you're ready to go looking for a fight. This is down to me. I'll go.'

'No.' A caring Letty put her arm affectionately around Logan's shoulders as Rosie brought Meade a full glass of whiskey.

Gratefully downing the drink, Meade said, 'There's no point in anyone doing anything until Casson gets back.'

'If Casson gets back,' Basso said pessimistically and wrongly, as they heard the outer door open and footsteps in the hall before a heated Casson entered the room.

'You get the coyote who shot Meade, Charles?' Logan eagerly asked.

'No sign of him, Dan,' Casson excitedly replied, his voice going up an octave as he shocked them all with an announcement. 'What I did find was close on a thousand head of DL cattle close to the Running M ranch house.

They're in a rope corral down in Amarillo Valley.'

'Are you sure of this, Casson?' Meade asked, aware of the difficulty in distinguishing brands at night.

'Of course he's sure,' Dan Logan snorted.

'I saw them with my own eyes, Meade, and Reg Lester was with me.'

'I said all along it was Buck Woodward,' Logan muttered angrily. 'Now we know, it's time to settle this once and for all.'

'I'll ride out there at first light,' Meade said.

'This calls for more'n one man, badge or no badge,' Logan grumbled.

'I'm advising you, Dan, no, gosh darn it, I'm telling you.' Moses Basso wagged a warning finger at the old man. 'You leave this to Henry Meade.'

Dan Logan made no reply.

9

Charles Casson had been telling the truth. There were no cattle there now, but there had been. The golden sunshine of early morning was searching out the canyons and gullies on the westerly side of the valley. Meade walked on ground that had recently been churned up by hundreds of hoofs. With his injured leg causing him no problems, he paced in widening circles until he came across the holes made by the posts of a temporary corral. Confirming what Casson had seen answered one question but posed many more. The DL foreman had been confident that the herd he had come across was made up solely of Dan Logan's cows. Why would Woodward separate DL cows from a rustled herd that probably included an equal number of Three Cs cattle? For what reason would he have brought the beef here, just a few miles from the Running M ranch house, and then moved them away again?

Something was very wrong about this, but Meade couldn't figure what it was. Widening his search as the sun rose higher to give him more light, he studied the ground intently. His task was made more difficult by not really knowing what he was looking for. Whatever it was, and he felt that the answer would eventually come to him, he didn't find it.

His only reasonable course of action seemed to be to follow the trail left by the stolen cattle. Going back to his horse, Meade reached both hands up to grasp the saddle, then paused to do some thinking. Tilting his head back he looked up at a red and gold-streaked dawn sky as if hoping to find the answers he sought written across it. There was nothing there. He already knew what he had to do, which was ride on into the Running M and confront

Buck Woodward with what was not real evidence.

He was up in the saddle when his name was shouted on the light breeze of morning. Turning he saw Letty coming riding down a grey sage-and-grease-wood-dotted slope to head for him. She was shouting as she came, but the wind generated by her galloping horse snatched her words away. Jerking the buckskin she rode to its haunches, she slid out of the saddle. There was a light covering of dust on her blue silk shirt and khaki riding skirt. The effort of the ride had made her pretty face as red as the flame-coloured scarf she had knotted around her throat.

'Myrtle sent me, Henry. She's in a terrible state, terrified of being left all alone in the world.'

Grasping the girl by the shoulders in an attempt at steadying her, Meade asked, 'What's happened, Letty?'

'It's old Dan,' she said, fighting for breath taken from her by the fast ride and a rising panic. 'He sent word to

Buck Woodward to meet him in town. Then he rode out for Tolula with Casson and the whole DL crew, all of them carrying rifles, Henry.'

'Was Cass Gore with them?'

The question that was important to him meant nothing to a frowning Letty. She said. 'I don't know who that is.'

'No, you wouldn't. I'm sorry,' Meade accepted that it was a silly question to ask her. Gore was one of the niggling half-questions lurking in the back of his mind. He remembered that the range detective had left the Faro Wheel before him the previous evening, but the significance of that eluded him as yet. 'I guess that I'd better head for town mighty quick. You go back to the ranch and stay with the old lady, Letty.'

'No.' She shook a determined head. 'I won't let you go alone, Henry. You try to stop it and you'll be caught in the middle. Dan Logan was really angry; in a terrible rage.'

Up in the saddle, aware that he

couldn't stop her going into Tolula with him, he said, 'When we hit town, Letty, and I find where Logan and Woodward are at, I don't want you anywhere near them.'

Making no reply, she mounted up and rode along at his side. Glancing at her as they went up an easy slope, noticing the strain on her lovely face, he remarked grimly, 'We didn't know what we were letting ourselves in for when we came to Tolula, Letty.'

'And it is all for nothing,' she said sadly.

'I wouldn't say that.' He managed a sideways smile for her. 'I guess I'll find a way of keeping Logan and Woodward apart, then we can go ahead as planned.'

'No, Henry, it's all over,' she argued, reining her horse close to his. 'It has nothing to do with this war between them. You see, Sheriff Basso knows that I'm not the Logans' grandchild.'

'How can he know that? Even you don't know who your parents were.'

'I do now,' she told him unhappily, 'Moses Basso told me.'

This was a stroke of unexpected bad luck. The odds against someone knowing Letty Dale's origin had to be many thousands to one. Neither was it a situation that could be solved with a gun or a bribe. Meade respected the sheriff too much to try the former, and Basso was too good a man to be interested in the latter.

'What does Basso say about it?' he enquired dully.

'He says that he won't let us fool Dan and Myrtle Logan.'

'There might still be a way,' Meade managed to say, though he now saw the situation as a hopeless one. A dream that would forever remain out of reach.

'I don't think so, Henry.'

'We'll talk about it when this business is settled,' he told her as they topped a rise and the outer buildings of the town came into view.

The sun had ridden higher now,

beating down with a relentless fierceness out of a tinny sky. These torrid conditions added to Meade's worries. Intense heat shortened the tempers of men and raised their passions to dangerous heights.

They paused for a moment in a little grove, beside an infinitesimal stream that added illusion to the sense of coolness. Overhead, the trees whispered in deep tones as a heated breeze stirred them. Meade was confounded by a situation that had innocuously developed and was now about to engulf him. He was about to put his life on the line to save people he'd only known for a very short time.

Apparently disturbed by similar thinking, Letty asked. 'How did we get drawn in to this, Henry?'

'It sure beats me.'

'I feel that we don't have any choice,' she frowned.

'I don't reckon we do,' Meade agreed. 'Come on, or it will be over before we hit town.'

The main street of Tolula was deserted when they rode in. It was as if the whole place had gone into advance mourning. The saloon was closed, and even Ikey Kindler seemed to have shut up his store. But he came out through a half-open door as they neared, hobbling over fast to halt Meade's horse by grasping the bridle.

'I'm sure glad you've turned up, Meade,' the storekeeper said with his habitual funereal expression on his face. 'Dan Logan's madder'n a rattler with its head stoved in, and I heard Buck Woodward ain't about to back down. They're down at the bottom of town, on Delano Flat.'

Meade knew the place. Like so many other western towns, Tolula had been built on a shelf of barren land. Its first settlers had built as far to the north as possible, leaving a long stretch of the shelf vacant for when the time came for the town to expand. It made an ideal arena.

‘Woodward got his men with him, Kindler?’

‘Every danged one of ’em, all armed to the teeth,’ the storekeeper replied. ‘They were here long before Dan rode in. Terrified Mrs Kindler, they did, prowling the town in twos and threes, on the prod, looking for trouble. That’s why all the townsfolk went in and locked and bolted their doors.’

Aware of countless staring eyes somewhere inside of the blind windows that lined the street, Meade paused to get as much of the situation as possible straight in his mind.

He asked Kindler, ‘Where’s Moses Basso?’

‘Sheriff’s down there with ’em, but he ain’t in no fit condition to do anything, if there was anything to be done, which there ain’t.’

Reaching down to grasp Kindler’s wrist, freeing his hand from the reins, Meade dug in his heels, letting the movement of the chestnut nudge the storekeeper aside as he and Letty moved on down the street.

The last building on the right side of the street was a long-defunct express company office. Slowing the pace of his horse, with Letty doing the same, Meade edged round the corner before reining up.

Two long lines of stationary horsemen faced each other, separated by some twenty-five yards. In the middle of one line was Dan Logan, with Charles Casson at his side. They both held rifles rising up at an angle from where the stocks rested on their saddlehorns. All the DL hands held rifles in the same way, as did the Running M cowboys in the opposing line-up. Directly across from Logan was a grim-faced Buck Woodward. Moses Basso stood at the far end, made diminutive by distance, his pose betraying his indecision.

Meade was scanning the line of DL riders for a sight of Cass Gore, before seeing him close by on foot, leaning his back against the wall of the express office as he rolled a cigarette. Dismounting, Meade went over to the range detective, Letty walking at his side.

'This sure isn't a happy situation, Meade,' Gore observed, finishing his cigarette and placing it in his mouth. 'Reminds me of a dog I had one-time, as a boy. Miserable cur he was, with teeth like razors.'

Unable to discover a connection between two small armies facing each other, and a dog with sharp teeth, an irritated Meade told Gore so.

'That's because you haven't heard the story,' Gore spoke patiently. 'I had me this job, see, delivering groceries for the local store. Rex, that was my dog, used to go along with me, walking at my heels like he was trailing a bear.'

This out-of-character loquaciousness Gore was showing, annoyed Meade further. He asked brusquely, 'Is there a point to this, Gore?'

Gore, once again exhibiting his

patience, said, 'Sure is. One day we met this other dog on the street. Peculiar looking animal he was. I can see that mutt now. It was as black as night except for a belt of white that came up over its neck and head and ran down between his forelegs. Anyhow, Rex and this strange dog just stood there glaring at each other. I was in a hurry, with groceries to drop off at various places. Deciding to break them up, I put my arm in between them.'

'What happened?' A curious Letty had to clear her throat before she could ask.

'Both the strange dog and Rex bit my arm through to the bone, miss.'

Meade said, 'So you're telling me, Gore . . . ?'

'That if you put yourself between these men here you're sure as shooting going to be bit by both sides.'

Shrugging off this advice, Meade said, 'Something has to be done.'

'You figured out which one is right and which one is wrong, Meade?'

'No, have you?' Meade queried.

'Could be they've both got it wrong,' was Gore's enigmatic answer.

Reluctant to waste more time, Meade ordered Letty to remain where she was. Going back to his horse, he climbed up into the saddle and moved slowly towards the avenue formed by the rows of mounted men. He didn't look back as Cass Gore called to him.

'You ride in there, Meade, and I won't back you up.'

'I didn't ask you to,' Meade replied, and rode on.

There was a faint stirring on both sides as he rode between the two ranks. He kept going, coming up to where Logan and Woodward were staring at each other. Without taking his eyes from Woodward, Dan Logan spoke in harsh tones to Meade.

'You've no part in this quarrel, Meade. You just ride on out to the ranch and take care of Myrtle till I get back.'

'Maybe you won't be going back,

Dan,' Meade said bluntly.

'Then so be it, Meade. At least I'll have done what I should have done the first day Buck Woodward rode into Tolula.'

'I think you've got it wrong, Dan.'

'You know better than that, Meade,' Charles Casson put in from where he sat his horse at Logan's side.

'I *know* you got it wrong, Henry,' Logan said, almost friendly-like, 'so, as I said, you ride on out to the DL, you've no business here.'

Drawing his rifle and laying it across the saddlehorn in front of him, Meade said, 'I'm here as a deputy sheriff, and you are a fool, Logan.'

'No one has ever called me a fool and lived to boast about it,' Dan Logan said, rage switching his gaze from Buck Woodward to Meade. 'Now I wouldn't feel bad about killing you. Get riding, Meade, or I'll blast you out of my way with this here rifle.'

'He means what he says, Henry, just ride back out of the way.' Moses Basso shouted advice from where he stood.

Buck Woodward spoke then for the first time. 'I like your guts, Meade, but this old guy is plumb loco. Maybe he'll kill me, maybe he won't, but there ain't no doubt he's going to shoot you if you don't hit the breeze.'

Probably Woodward spoke the truth, but Meade didn't intend to back away. He saw Casson's eyes fix on something, or someone, behind him, and heard the DL foreman ask, 'Why are you butting into this?'

Still keeping a wary eye on Logan, Meade leaned back a little and turned his head slightly to see Cass Gore standing nearby. Despite his declaration of non-assistance, the range detective had walked up soft-footed to side Meade.

'I'm just here to say, Casson,' Gore said flatly, 'that this little stand-off has come to an end. Any one of you make the slightest move, and me'n Meade will kill you, Casson, Dan Logan and Buck Woodward.'

The audacity of what Gore had said, and the superb logic behind it staggered Meade. This way there could be no winners. With both sides guaranteed as losers there was no longer any point to the confrontation. But Dan Logan hadn't been influenced by Cass Gore's threat.

Lifting his rifle a little, he said, 'If that's how it's got to be, then I'll die happy knowing that Woodward is finished, too, and I still have a ranch to give to my grandchild.'

These words brought all the danger and tension back into play. Meade, depending on Gore, was waiting for the range detective to say something, when the sound of hoofbeats came from the town end of the line-up of opposing forces. All heads turned to see Rosie Kirby riding up slowly, leading a horse on which sat a man with his hands tied behind his back. As Rosie drew nearer, Meade recognized her captive as Lester, the young cowboy who had been with Casson the previous evening.

'Hear me, Dan Logan, you old hothead,' Rosie Kirby said, chin held high, her long hair flowing from under a narrow-brimmed stetson, 'before you get to regret blasting away. My boys came upon a band of rustlers herding a bunch of your beef out towards Kline Canyon. The others got away, but they got this lad from the DL.'

That had to be the cows Casson had come across on Running M land. Meade was beginning to put things together in his head when he heard an angry roar from Casson.

'Snakes alive! Dan, we've been betrayed by one of our own,' the ramrod exclaimed in disgust, dismounting and stepping out of the line of horses to put his rifle to his shoulder and aim it at a quaking Lester.

The sequence that followed was blurred by its speed. Gore drew the gun at his right hip and fired. The rifle, its stock shattering, was knocked out of Casson's grasp, leaving him to shake his stinging hands.

Cass Gore, his gun back in its holster so fast that it might never have been drawn, said, 'There'll be no necktie party here, Casson. Deputy Meade's the law, and he'll take care of Lester.'

Lowering his head as if in agreement with this, Casson suddenly sprang to life, going for his holstered. 45. But the gun at Gore's left hip appeared in his hand as if by a miracle. Not having cleared leather, Casson let go of his gun and held his hand clear as a token of surrender.

'I don't rightly know what's taking place here,' Logan said, 'but you take the boys back to the DL, Charles. Are you going to hold Lester, Henry?'

'I'll take him down to the jail,' Sheriff Basso walked up to say.

Meade turned to the Running M rancher. 'Seems like it's all over here, Woodward. You want to push the argument any further?'

'I wasn't arguing in the first place, Meade,' Woodward answered. 'I'm happy to lead my boys quietly out of town.'

'Good,' Meade acknowledged the rancher's co-operation with a wave of his arm. As the Running M riders moved away, Meade remarked to Gore, 'It could be that you're as fast as me, but I'm sure glad I don't have to find out right now.'

'You'd be fine,' Gore told him, keeping a poker face. 'There's enough horses here to help you out.' Then his voice sharpened. 'Take care of Lester, Meade, he'll be your star witness.'

'Against Charles Casson?'

Giving him an appreciative look, Gore said, 'I thought you'd catch on. Casson's running the rustling gang, which is why he didn't touch Running M stock. He wanted to throw suspicion on Woodward. He was going to gun Lester down just now because he's scared the boy will split on him.'

'I thought Casson was making himself look good in Logan's eyes,' Meade confessed ruefully. 'That's going to be the hardest part of it all, telling old Dan.'

'I'll leave that to you,' an unsympathetic Gore announced. 'But be quick about it, Henry. Casson's got twenty real hard men minding the rustled beef out at Kline Canyon. You and me had better ride out there tonight and take a look-see.'

10

In a dismal dawn, Meade and Gore rode back to the DL. It had been a long night in which their worst fears had been confirmed. The treacherous Casson had chosen the location for the rustled herd wisely. Kline Canyon was a natural fortress that could be held indefinitely by one man with enough ammunition. It would take a well-planned campaign to get into the canyon to retrieve the stolen cattle.

'Charles Casson intended to bring Rosie Kirby and Dan Logan to their knees, then buy them both out at a bargain price,' Cass Gore commented as he and Meade topped a rise and saw the DL ranch house down below, ghost-like in the swirling mist. 'You put the coyote among the chickens when you rode in with that girl. Logan wouldn't give up the ranch when he had a grandchild to leave it to, and he saw you and your gun as a way of saving the place, Henry.'

Meade could understand how he had upset Casson's plans, but he pointed out to Gore, 'It wasn't Casson who bushwhacked me that night.'

'Somebody fired the shot on his orders. Casson put himself in the clear by helping you.' Gore put into words what Meade at the same time deduced. Gore pointed to the house. 'There's Rosie Kirby's horse.'

Rosie came to meet them, surprising Meade by embracing him warmly. He asked the approaching Dan Logan, 'Is Casson here, Dan?'

'He'd ridden out when I got back last night, Henry. I reckon as how he's hunting down them rustlers. What have you boys learned?'

'They're holding the cattle in Kline Canyon,' Gore said, going on to save Meade a dreaded task. 'Sorry, Logan, but Charles Casson is at the head of the rustling gang.'

Meade could tell that Dan Logan was shaken to the core by the betrayal. But the tough old rancher covered his hurt well. He said hollowly, 'I'll get all the hands saddled up.'

'It isn't that simple,' Meade cautioned. 'You'll be sending cowpunchers out against at least twenty fast guns, Dan.'

'I'll fetch my crew, and I reckon Buck Woodward will help out,' Rosie Kirby said. About to object, Logan then shrugged resignedly.

'Weight of numbers won't do it. The only way in is a narrow pass,' Meade said. Suddenly worried, he asked, 'Where's Letty?'

'Off on the buckskin for her regular morning ride.'

Meade exchanged anxious glances with Gore, who said tersely, 'Casson.'

'Is Letty in danger?' Rosie asked.

'You shouldn't have let her go, Logan,' Meade said angrily.

'Have you ever tried to stop that girl doing something when she's made up her mind?' Logan retorted.

'What's going on?' a now seriously perturbed Rosie demanded an answer.

'Casson could use the girl as a hostage and hold us off while he gets all the rustled beef away,' Gore replied.

'I'm going out to find her,' Meade shouted over his shoulder, as he ran to his horse.

'It'll take two of us, Henry,' Gore called to him, giving Logan and Rosie Kirby an order before he, too, hurried to his horse. 'Get your men together and ride out. Wait just this side of Kline Canyon for me and Meade.'

The necessity to ride slowly so as to study the ground made both Meade and Gore impatient. Far ahead a long white mass of vapour from the valleys writhed into nothingness as the rays of the sun grew warmer. They passed over a green space and began to descend a long slope of naked earth.

'How are you at tracking, Henry?' Gore asked.

'As good as any other man, I guess.'

'That means you're better than me,' Gore conceded, straightening up in his saddle, leaving Meade to study the ground.

They rode over a little hillock and into a wide canyon. Then it narrowed. Sheer, rocky walls hemmed them in on both sides. For a long time the canyon was empty, and Meade slowed his horse because a stretch of hard ground made tracking impossible. Then both men spotted a splash of brown, which was a saddled horse grazing among the bushes.

'It's Letty's buckskin, gone lame again,' Meade said, when they had dismounted to examine the horse. He looked at the ground around them, reading the signs carefully before telling Gore, 'Four horses, so Casson must have met up with some of his gang and taken Letty. Looks like they're heading for Kline Canyon.'

'Then we'd better get riding, Henry.'

They rode fast then. There was a chance to stop Casson and rescue the girl if they could catch them up before they reached Kline Canyon. Then it could be left to the cowhands of the DL and the Three Cs to recover the stolen herd. But if Casson made it to the canyon before them, then with Letty as a hostage he could hold them off until the herd had been moved on.

Casson and Letty were nowhere to be seen as they rode up out of a valley floor to see the forbiddingly narrow entrance of Kline Canyon up ahead. Meade knew that the rustlers would have someone with a rifle high up on one of the precipitous cliffs that formed the sides of the canyon. Probably Casson himself would have stayed, totally secure because he now had Letty to use as a shield.

'What we'd better — ' Meade started saying just before the report of a rifle came from up on the cliff to their right.

Gore was hit. He was knocked clean out of the saddle, crashing to the ground in the slack-bodied way of a dead or unconscious man. But he was conscious as Meade reined his horse near and prepared to dismount, asking, 'Are you hurt bad, Cass?'

Through teeth clenched to hold off pain, Gore said, 'I don't know, and you haven't got time to find out. Go get him, Henry, before he puts a hole through your head.'

Taking the advice, though reluctant to leave the injured Gore, Meade lay flat against the neck of his chestnut horse as he rode at a gallop towards the cliff. Two shots were fired at him. The first went whining past close to his head, while the second harmlessly kicked up dirt in front of the horse.

Dismounting, Meade scrambled up a grassy rise leading up to an overhanging cliff. Taking his rifle with him was ruled out as he needed both hands to get fingerholds in the rock. He went up gradually, gravity pulling at him, the overhang forcing him to lean back, fingers hurting and boots slipping and scraping on the jagged rock as he fought to gain footholds. There was a shelf some thirty feet above him, and he struggled on upwards. The going was arduous. Straining, sweating, the ground far below becoming more dizzying as the length of the drop increased.

Thankfully reaching the ledge, he grasped it with both hands. Arms aching, he pulled himself up. There was a shot from above. A bullet smacked against the rock close to his head, splinters of sharp stone slashing his face. Blinded by dust, Meade instinctively went to knuckle his sore eyes, an action that made him drop so that his body hung at an angle, supported only by one hand.

With the drag on his arm causing pain beyond endurance, Meade swung his other hand up to regain a grip. Blinking rapidly, he partially cleared his sight. Bending his neck back, he looked up. Standing on the ledge to his left, a short distance in from the edge, was a huge boulder that would provide him with cover. Moving along hand over hand, his body unfeeling now and his brain numb, he pulled himself up onto the shelf. Crouching behind the boulder he fingered the dust from his eyes and wiped blood from his lacerated face, as he allowed time for his strength to return.

Twice he flinched as slugs hit the rock. Peering cautiously out, he saw Casson. The former DL foreman was beside a large opening in the cliff face, turning his back towards Meade as he started to climb to a higher position, hampered by the rifle he clutched in his right hand.

Drawing his .45, Meade fired quickly from the hip. His bullet drilled Casson's right forearm. Falling back down on to the ledge, dropping his rifle, Casson went at a crouch towards the cave opening. Meade, wanting to get to him before he disappeared, came out from behind the rock at a run, but halted, mystified, as he saw Casson was still outside the cave, kneeling to concentrate on some task.

Suddenly swinging round, coming up on to his haunches, a Colt .44 held in his left hand, Casson levelled the gun at Meade, calling hoarsely. 'Hold it right there, Meade. The Dale girl's in the cave behind me. Whether she lives or dies is up to you. Put down your gun.'

Bending a knee, a disappointed Meade laid his .45 on the ledge and straightened up. Casson had kept him covered all the time, but Meade was quick to notice that the DL's erstwhile ramrod was not naturally lefthanded, and blood was running freely down over his right hand.

Deciding he had to take a chance, Meade rushed at Casson. Casson fired, the bullet tore at the flesh on Meade's right side, just below the armpit. The impact spun him round so that he fell to one knee with his back to Casson. Hearing the hammer of Casson's gun pulled back, Meade dropped onto his buttocks, using them to pivot himself round. He was close enough to lash out with his right foot to kick the gun out of Casson's hand.

They both scrambled for the weapon. Casson's weight was on top of Meade, who wriggled a knee into position. Bringing the knee up, he drove it with force into Casson's face, shattering the man's nose and cheekbones. But Casson was strong and determined. Swinging Meade on to his back, he straddled him, blood dropping from his injured face, his speech snuffling as he said. 'None of us will get the DL, Meade. You haven't saved the girl. All three of us are about to die.'

At first baffled by this, Meade was suddenly horrified to hear a sizzling sound behind him. Casson had brought dynamite up here to block the pass, and had lit the fuse before Meade had shot him. Bending his head back, straining sore eyes, Meade saw the long, thin fuse trailing into the cave, a sparking, sizzling flame travelling along it. Depending on how much dynamite had been primed there might be a chance of survival out here. But Letty was doomed in the cave.

Having retrieved his gun, Casson raised it high in his left hand, ready to bring it down hard on Meade's head. Looking at Casson's right forearm, the sleeve of which was soaked with blood halfway down, Meade realized that his bullet must have shattered the bones. He snaked out a hand to grab the forearm right on the wound and dig his fingers in hard.

Pain made Casson gasp and writhe. Taking advantage of the brief respite this afforded him, Meade threw his opponent off him. Scrambling to his feet, Meade ran towards the ever-shortening fuse. But Casson ran and jumped on his back. The two of them crashed down on to the rock ledge, with Meade underneath, face down.

Stretching out his hand, Meade's fingers were just inches from the fuse when Casson caught his wrist, pulling his arm back. Aware that there were only minutes to go before the cliff-face exploded, Meade drove his right elbow back blindly. It crashed into Casson's already smashed face, sending him flying backwards.

Diving to pick up his own gun, Meade used it to smash Casson across the face with it as he was rising to his feet. Staggering back, Casson released a hoarse scream as he toppled back off the ledge.

Satisfied that Casson had gone over, Meade ran to the mouth of the cave, having to enter a few feet to stamp on the lighted fuse and put it out. Adjusting his eyes to the darkness inside, Meade gave up and hurried out when he heard a cry.

'Help!'

Charles Casson was hanging on to the edge of the cliff with his one good hand. Distorted by injury and covered in blood, his face was still able to register abject fear.

'Help me! For God's sake help me, Meade.'

As Meade watched, Casson's fingers slowly slipped from the rim of the shelf.

With a long scream of terror, he dropped like a stone.

A little shaken by what he had witnessed, Meade took a deep breath and went into the cave. In the dim interior he found Letty Dale in a corner, bound hand and foot and so frightened that she had little grasp of what was going on. Cringing from Meade at first, she then recognized him and was able to relax a little. Untying her, he helped her to her feet and held her until circulation returned to her arms and legs.

'Casson?' she enquired weakly.

'Don't worry about Casson,' Meade advised.

'He's dead, isn't he?' she guessed. 'Did you kill him, Henry?'

'Not exactly,' he said in what was a half answer. 'Come on, we'd better move. I've got to find a way down from here.'

'We can go down the way Casson brought me up.'

Following her down, Meade, wanting

to save her from the sight of Casson's body, left her at the entrance to the canyon while he went round the side to where he had left his horse. The broken remains of Casson, snapped, jagged bones poking whitely through red flesh, lay not far away. Glancing at it, just once, Meade mounted up and rode to collect Letty. He was anxious to get back to where he had left Cass Gore. Hoping against hope that he would find the range detective alive.

With Letty riding up behind him on the chestnut, they met Dan Logan, Rosie Kirby, and Buck Woodward riding ahead of an army made up of hands from all three ranches.

'Thank the Lord you saved her, Henry,' Logan said. His deep and confused feelings over his former ramrod were evident when he asked a one-word question. 'Casson?'

'Casson's dead, Dan,' Meade, sorry for the old cattleman, answered. 'The canyon's wide open for you to ride in and fetch your cattle.'

Rosie Kirby called to him from where she sat in the saddle. 'Me and Dan owe you a lot, Henry. I hope that you'll be at the DL when we ride back.'

Not certain that he would be there, Meade didn't reply. Though he had perhaps earned the reward in a different way from the original intention, he was aware that Letty wouldn't want to stay to be exposed as a fraud by the honest Sheriff Basso.

'Did you come across Cass Gore when you rode in?' he asked worriedly.

'I'm here, Henry.'

Gore, his right arm in a sling and his shirt bloodied, rode forward from among the ranks of the cowboys.

'It's great to see you, Cass,' a relieved Meade said.

'I don't doubt it,' Gore grinned, pointing to his injured arm and shoulder. 'This is your chance, Henry. You shouldn't even need a horse to help you.'

'I think we can bury that feud here and now,' Meade offered.

'I reckon you're right, Henry,' Gore smiled.

'We must waste no more time,' Dan Logan said. 'Henry, take one of the spare horses for Letty, and the two of you get back to the ranch. When I return I'll have good news for you both.'

The old man's enthusiasm embarrassed and humbled Letty and Meade as they rode back towards the DL. Neither spoke for some time, and it was Letty who broke the silence between them.

'What do we do, Henry, get our things and leave to avoid old Dan when he gets back?'

Meade was dubious. 'We face him, Letty, tough though it will be, and it'll all be over. If we run away, the shame of it will stay with us for the rest of our lives.'

'Right.' She made an attempt at speaking firmly. 'I don't think I could have gone through with it if the sheriff hadn't found out. We'll face up to it, but we'll take no money from Dan Logan.'

'I don't think he'll be about to give us any,' Meade wryly remarked.

They went back to being silent after that exchange, not speaking again until they were at the ranch and turning their horses loose in the corral. It was late afternoon, and Letty announced that she was going up to sit with Myrtle Logan for a while. Meade was aware how sad she was, close to tears, knowing that this was the last time she would spend with the old lady she had become so fond of.

'Will you tell her the truth?' Meade asked.

'No,' she replied with a shake of her head. 'I'll leave that to Dan. I know it's cowardly, but I couldn't bear to see her hurt.'

More than an hour passed before a tearful Letty came back down the stairs. She stood for a long time absently looking out of the french windows of the Logans' lounge. Meade didn't know what to say, so he stayed quiet.

Then she turned to take a step towards him and stood looking earnestly up into his eyes. 'I'm terribly mixed up, Henry. I would love to stay here at the DL, but even if that was possible, I wouldn't want you to leave.'

Her stated interest in him focused the almost abstract thoughts he'd recently had of her. Everything was becoming too complicated. He tried to shake off his feelings, asking her a question that would keep the conversation neutral.

'Where will you go, Letty?'

'I don't know,' she said unhappily. 'The only road I know is the one back to Raimondo and Nelly Kierney.'

Feeling for her, Meade said, 'I'm real sorry, Letty. I shouldn't have raised your hopes the way I did, shouldn't have taken you from Raimondo.'

'I'm glad that you did, but it's going to be hard saying goodbye to the Logans, and harder still to leave you,' she said with a sigh. 'When do you think they'll get back?'

'Mid-morning at the earliest,' Meade predicted.

It was, in fact, noon when Dan Logan, Rosie Kirby, Buck Woodward and Cass Gore rode in, all of them jubilant. Letty had dozed fitfully in a chair, but Meade had been awake all night, dreading the coming of a day in which the ambitions of both of them would be crushed. Yet during that long night he learned that, like Letty, he couldn't have continued to live a lie.

'Got every man-jack of them, Henry,' an elated Logan called when Letty and Meade walked out to meet the four riders. 'Them rustlers won't be giving anyone else any trouble. All the boys are safe, too. Just Jacky Lewton from Buck's place got hit, but that was only a nicked ear that bled one whole lot.'

'Can we speak with you for a moment, Dan?' Meade asked as Logan and the others dismounted.

Nodding assent, Dan Logan called to the others. 'Go on into the house, folks, and chase up that lazy cook of mine. Tell him to rustle us up some grub, *muy pronto*.'

Logan then turned to them, his lined face apprehensive more than worried. 'Say what you have to say, Henry.'

With only a slight hesitation, Meade said, 'Both me and Letty have something to tell you before Moses Basso gets around — '

'Moses Basso!' Logan snorted. 'That man takes me for a godamned fool. I knew you weren't who you claimed to be, girl, right from the start. I confess that I fooled myself for a while, but I ain't plumb loco the way that sheriff thinks I am.'

'You've known all along!' a white-faced Letty gasped. 'I'm sorry . . . '

'Sorry! Sorry!' Dan Logan became animated. 'Folk don't have no choice but to be stuck with their relatives. I've been given a rare chance to pick my own kin, and I couldn't ask for a finer granddaughter than you, Letty.'

Overcome with emotion, an uncertain smile flickering at the corners of her mouth. 'You mean . . . ?'

'I mean that you're my grandchild,' Dan Logan smiled, 'and it'll be kinder of all three of us if Myrtle never learns there was any doubt.'

'She won't find out from either Henry or me,' a delighted Letty was saying as Rosie Kirby came out of the house and walked over to them.

'Well, Henry Meade,' Rosie said, 'you've sure proved yourself to all of us. Now, what do you say to becoming ramrod of the Three Cs?'

'No chance, Rosie,' Letty smiled happily and sweetly. 'Henry's staying here to be foreman of the DL.'

This came to Meade as a surprise. But it sounded like a brilliant idea to him. His answer was to put an arm round Letty's shoulders and hug her to him.